About the Author

Les Fields is a retired South Pacific underwater photographer, diving operator and resort owner. As founder of Aqua Trek Diving, his career was principally based in Fiji and focused on the company's specialty of shark diving. The broader scope of his work brought him to worldwide destinations. As a veteran of several Arctic dive expeditions, his range of underwater experience is unusual and diverse.

Derek Dell, Flash Before Your Eyes

Les Fields

Derek Dell, Flash Before Your Eyes

Olympia Publishers
London

www.olympiapublishers.com
OLYMPIA PAPERBACK EDITION

ISBN: 978-1-78830-419-1

This is a work of fiction.
Names, characters, places and incidents originate from the writer's
imagination. Any resemblance to actual persons, living or dead, is
purely coincidental.

First Published in 2019

Olympia Publishers
60 Cannon Street
London
EC4N 6NP

Printed in Great Britain

Dedication

To Dr. Wendell M. (Dell) Fields

Christmas in Paradise

Cook's Bay is a tranquil body located on the island of Moorea, French Polynesia. Captain Cook, after whom it was named, was a well-known pioneer of early South Pacific Island groups. In the eighteenth century Cook explored regions of the world never before visited by Europeans.

Since the days of Captain Cook, French Polynesia has grown and changed. From the main island of Tahiti through the outreach atolls and archipelagos, French Polynesia has moved gracefully into the twenty-first century. While other South Pacific Island nations have struggled with their independence, French Polynesia has rested comfortably in the care of Paris and the greatness of France. Moreover, the blend of European and Polynesian cultures results in people who are both attractive and sophisticated.

Added to the shocking beauty of the place, these are the reasons Derek and Juliet Dell chose Cook's Bay in Moorea as their South Pacific Island home. The island of Moorea is located just offshore from the FP's main island of Tahiti. The view of Moorea from Papeete (capital city) is both stunning and mindful of a convenient separation from busy Tahiti.

Their family neighborhood on Cook's Bay is characteristic of island living. People know one another. You can rely on your neighbor and most people consider themselves locals and friends. Even if you do not know a given person you have likely seen them around and there is an assumed comfort that permeates the area.

The house is a few miles from the ferry landing located right on the water. Everything about the architecture of island homes is centered on outdoor living. As such, the house's main living space includes a portion of the swimming pool that extends to the outside area, toward the beach. The beach itself is fine white sand, bleached by morning sun, warm until it meets the water's edge. It is the segue from indoor living to outdoor environment that blends the house with nature.

The place is fully equipped with the necessary Wi-Fi, big screen TV and other lounge toys of the day. Comfort is the key to the room's arrangement. Furniture is soft and accommodating, suitable for the needs of an aging Derek Dell's accumulated sprains, strains and bone breaks.

Artwork is important to the Dells. The house holds a combination of underwater photos, European sculpture and framed pieces reflecting South Pacific Island history. Enough work to cause you to pause while taking it all in. Art in the house tells stories. One's curiosity about the stories increases as more art is viewed. It is obvious that a significant portion of

Derek Dell's life was lived in the South Pacific. It is equally obvious that those years were a time of substantial adventure. Some of that adventure was known to Derek's family and friends, much of it entirely unknown.

All the family members are prideful cooks. Cooking is one of the many rituals practiced by Derek Dell. That means a gourmet kitchen for the house is essential. The kitchen is scrupulously populated with utensils, pots, pans and all manner of culinary tools. Juliet made certain there was ample granite counter-top space and professional level appliances.

Just outside the kitchen is a dining area with enough table space for family gatherings. The culture of the South Pacific, places strong emphasis on family. So do the Dells. Finally achieving a proper family environment was a long journey for Derek Dell.

The house provides the Dells with such an ideal island lifestyle, Derek named it "C-bay". To get a nickname from Derek Dell was a sign of unique importance. To him nicknames are several characteristics condensed into a simple defining phrase. C-bay was indeed many special things and a very special place.

The beach on this part of Cook's Bay is a white sand, soft grade, leading down to shallow warm waters. Teaming with activity, the shallows are an inviting entry to the ecosystem of the Bay's greater depths. This is where locals enjoy a day at the beach, a bit of spear fishing or possibly an outrigger paddle.

It is also where Derek Dell often begins another personal practice of early morning diving.

The dive might be free-diving, consisting of merely a snorkel, mask and fins, or perhaps full scuba gear. All dives will, of course, include an underwater camera to indulge Dell's passion for photo art.

Early morning is an active time in the ocean. When the darkness slowly surrenders to morning light, the ocean literally springs alive.

The nocturnal creatures are seeking shelter for the day to safely close a night of hunting and feeding. The day dwellers, on the other hand, are just beginning the same process. This is the time and place where nature's art can be captured on camera, or the evening dinner can be obtained on a Bola spear. It was always diver's choice.

Now over seventy years old, Dell is retired but had owned a scuba diving and underwater photography business in the South Pacific Island Republic of Fiji. In business in Fiji over thirty years, he sold the company and called it quits in 2009.

A bit of a pioneer himself, Derek Dell was best known for shark-wrangling skills practiced in his business, "Aqua Trek, Ocean Sports Adventures". Shark-wrangling is the management of sharks so as to present them for viewing and safe encounter. The audience is wide and varied. It ranges from tourist sport divers and scientists to professional photographers and film makers.

Dell, his partner Gilly (Gilroy Kelly) and their friend and master diver Api (Apisai Bati) introduced that activity to Fiji in the 1980s. The early days of the scuba diving business in Fiji often required a spread in the scope of diving services. That was how you survived.

It was Christmas time, a great opportunity for Derek and Juliet Dell to venture from their primary home in Northern California to C- bay. Juliet was a stunning woman. She first met Derek in late 2000. They were introduced by a common friend. Twenty years Dell's junior, she was his dream girl. Not only gorgeous and sexy, but fully able to run her life and business as an experienced professional. She was a natural for the island lifestyle. She loved the climate, wearing pareos and barefoot elegance. Most of all, she loved Derek Dell.

Derek and Juliet were very excited as their three daughters and son-in-law were coming to C-bay for the holidays. Even more exciting, their ten-year-old grandson Charlie was coming too. There is no doubt that Derek and Juliet Dell were preparing for their ideal family Christmas, an important part of this time of their lives.

The plane from Los Angeles was due to arrive at the airport in Papeete, early in the morning. The Dells took the first ferry from Moorea to Papeete on the big island of Tahiti. The ferry is a unique experience indeed. More of a yacht than a ferry, it features several big screen TVs broadcasting news and sporting events. The buffet of tasty French pastries, sliced fruit and baked goods is both healthy and sinful on the same table. Christmas brings out the best in any French pastry chef. Such was the case on the

Papeete Ferry. The main cabin air was thick with the smell of freshly baked products, European coffee and sweet fruit. The ocean was glassy smooth, the skies were clear and the mood was joyful. This was a recipe for great day in paradise!

As the craft eased into its Papeete slip a growing excitement came over the Dells. There was so much to share: not only the holiday family element of the gathering at C-bay but the unique ability of Derek to present the ocean and the island experience to his family.

Particularly important was teaching what he knew to grandson Charlie. Derek was very keen to teach Charlie all about the ocean and Charlie equally keen to learn. They were both most excited for this bonding experience. A television interviewer once referred to Derek as a "Dare-Devil Diver". That moment was a stain on Dell's reputation that stuck with him his entire career. The whole family often worried but only Juliet had the courage to ask, "Just exactly what the hell will you be teaching Charlie, Mr. Dare-Devil Diver?"

Derek replied with his notorious smile of confidence, stating, "Safety first, baby, safety first. That's how you live to my age in the ocean." Of course, no one believed him but, once again, charm and conviction saved Derek Dell from a moment of discomfort.

At the airport Derek and Juliet positioned themselves just outside the exit from customs/immigration. This was the first time the entire family had been together in the islands. There is a warm feeling that comes with welcoming loved ones to Tahiti.

Juliet is armed with leis, smiles and hugs. Her tropical pareo, thick long hair and deep tan produce a natural Polynesian appearance. Derek has summoned baggage handlers then staged himself behind Juliet. Dressed in a blue-toned Aloha shirt and light blue Armani slacks, Derek looks anxiously at the exit door. The greeting planned by the Dells demonstrates both love for their family and respect for the difficulty of their journey.

Showing respect is a staple of protocol for South Pacific people. Leis are meant to refresh a traveler after a long journey. Fragrance from plumeria flowers pleasantly opens your senses to a relaxed island pace. A tropical fruit drink accompanies the leis. Not only a sensory delight, the juice helps with dehydration that plagues people spending long periods of time on aircraft.

Whatever their physical condition after the ten-hour night flight from LA, the family's energy will spring alive when the exit doors open from arrival and the holidays begin in paradise.

The Festivities Begin!

Derek and Juliet arranged for the family to fly first class. This meant they would be quickly off the plane in the most rested condition. After what seemed like an eternity the exit door opened. First to burst out was Charlie. The apple of his grandmother's eye, Charlie rushed into her open arms. After a gripping hug, a flurry of face kissing and the presentation of a lei, Juliet finally let Charlie go. He quickly bounced over to Derek for more of the same. Next out were Charlie's parents, daughter Rachael and her husband Drake Bonner. Drake was lean and athletic. Derek looked forward to fishing with Drake, teaching him and Charlie to dive. It was Drake's first venture to the South Pacific and his travel fatigue was offset by his awe.

Derek immediately directed the luggage away from Drake and over to the waiting porters. With hands free both Rachael and Drake were able to engage Derek and Juliet in a warm island welcome.

The Dells are a blended family. Daughters Rachael and Torchy are from Juliet's first marriage. Derek's daughter Lydia is from his first marriage as well. Torchy (Trudeau) and Lydia (Dell) were the last family members off the aircraft. Derek Dell had raised

Lydia as a single dad. They had made many trips to the South Pacific together. Torchy, the youngest, was also new to French Polynesia. The excitement amongst all was notable, even admired with a smile by other debarking travelers.

"I'm having the luggage sent over to C-bay," said Dell. "Juliet and I need to head to the market place here in Papeete. It's the best place for fresh food. If you're too tired you can take the ferry with the porters and we'll meet you at C-bay. If not, join us, you'll love the market place." It was settled. All were heading to the market place. Experiencing Papeete's main market place is something unusual by any standard.

It is located in the business area near the docks. An enormous space, the market place is composed of numerous vendor tables where local products are sold. Area restaurants all purchased their supplies at the market place. One would expect to find colorful fruits and vegetables grown in the rich volcanic soil of the South Pacific. What is surprising, however, are the intense hues and shades of color. During his long diving career Derek Dell had seen many richly-colored coral reefs. Nothing he saw diving compared to the extreme color scale of the displayed products for sale at the market place. Your eyes actually tremble in their sockets. This phenomenon can occur when the eye must process a complex vision. Added to the ocular impact was the aroma that accompanied the various foods. The place was sensory overload.

Juliet was particularly interested in specialty

items she needed for her signature dish, poisson cru. This is a raw tuna dish soaked in a sauce of green onion, coconut milk and other, "secret" ingredients. "We do a similar dish in Fiji called kakoda (kakonda). Difference is we use a white fish, usually walu," said Derek. "I like Juliet's far better," he added.

"Of course you do," quipped Juliet. For a bunch of would-be chefs like the Dell family the Papeete market place was an absolute delight.

It is impossible for anyone to visit the market place and not exit hungry. By the time you have wandered down row after row of beauty and fragrance your mouth waters for the taste that must ultimately accompany the sights and smells you have savored. With all dispatch Derek sent the supplies to C-bay with the luggage and the group adjourned to Juliet and Derek's favorite marina restaurant, Michelle's.

Papeete dining is simply superb! There is an abundance of talented French chefs and their skills in crafting the local foods are tremendous. Derek settled for his favorite, mixed green salad topped with seared ahi tuna. Salads appealed to everyone after a visit to the market place. Michelle's made the dish specially for Derek. The salad included greens and fruits which satisfied his market place-born hunger. It was commonly believed that the best tuna found anywhere in the world came from French Polynesia. It was superbly grilled and fan displayed on the salad. Derek Dell was in culinary heaven. By the time Derek and Chef Michelle had finished their conversation about the dish, everyone at the table had to have it as well. Some substituted grilled prawns for the ahi. It seems the market place had the same effect on everyone in the family.

Of course, the constant need to hydrate in the South Pacific was conquered by Derek Dell through Tahitian beer called Hinano. "Hydration in tropical climates is important," lectured Dell. Perhaps two Hinanos would be better. Drake joined Derek with a Hinano. The others shared a bottle of Jadot Pouilly Fuisse. Charlie had a combination papaya/mango juice.

From the restaurant you can see the nearby island of Moorea quite well. Anticipation grew as Derek and Juliet told the family of Moorea's history and details of life at C-bay. Lunch was a leisurely event of over two hours. Good conversation and good food made meals a very important time for Juliet and Derek. Everyone at the table was in a mild state of disbelief. Sitting there looking at Moorea while dining in paradise was an amazing reality. Even Charlie wasn't fidgety as ten-year-olds tend to be.

He was so curious about the ocean, he couldn't take his eyes off it. "Are you gonna teach me to dive, Poppy?" asked Charlie. Poppy was his nickname for Derek.

"You're darn right I am," said Dell. "First you'll learn to snorkel and free dive. That's where you start. Once you get that down I'll introduce you to SCUBA diving," Dell proudly stated.

"What does SCUBA mean, Poppy?" asked Charlie.

"SCUBA stands for Self Contained Underwater Breathing Apparatus," Dell answered. "Lydia, will you help me?" Derek asked.

"Sure, Dad, I'll be happy to help," she said. Lydia loved the ocean and had grown very comfortable in it during the years she traveled with her dad from San Francisco to Fiji. She also loved kids. No question, she would be of great assistance in teaching all the family members about the ocean and how to best enjoy it.

"Okay, guys," said Dell. "We've got an hour before the next ferry to Moorea. If you need anything like shampoo or sun protection there's a drug store just a block over to the right. I need a few things so let's head out." The luggage and provisions from the market place would be waiting at C-bay so there was no hurry. The family cruised the streets of Papeete, shopping for small things feeling like excited tourists.

Everywhere they went, shop keepers admired Juliet's Tahitian pearls. A stunning set of earrings complemented the necklace which included clustered diamonds to highlight the black pearls. All the daughters looked forward to obtaining something similar. Tahitian black pearls are unique to French Polynesia. Each shop offered different pearls with various settings or chains. It was clear that the stroll had changed from picking up a few toiletries to gawking in awe over the amazing pearls found in the shops of Papeete.

Sadly, time had come to leave the pearls and catch

the ferry. There would be ample time to shop as the holiday season in Tahiti carried on. Only a short walk from the shopping area the Dell family strolled aboard the ferry. Surprised by its upscale ambiance, the Donners and Torchy were all smiles and enjoying the comforts. Lydia had experienced the crossing before but still loved the hour-plus ride. Everyone settled in for the brief, smooth sail to Moorea. For Derek and Drake, another Hinano would punctuate the trip.

When the boat arrived at the ferry landing in Moorea there was always a scramble for the limited number of taxis. Knowing this, Derek had made arrangements with a van transport. After a short but stunning drive down the coast the van arrived at C-bay.

C-bay only had two bedrooms. Derek had made a trade with his next-door neighbor Tico. Derek and Juliet's primary residence was a place called Miracle Mountain Ranch. MMR had a colorful history in the Dell's past. During Derek and Juliet's early years MMR served as a ranch for kids with cancer. The Dells created a place where families of cancer-stricken children could spend a week enjoying ranch activities as a close-knit family. It is located in Northern California. The town of Willits is in Mendocino County. In itself MMR was one of the more beautiful properties imaginable. It was easy to persuade Tico to take his family for a once-in-a-lifetime Christmas in Redwoods of Northern California. It was all set. The Donners would stay at Tico's while Lydia and Torchy shared the spare bedroom at C-bay. All were happy.

Darkness comes early in December on Moorea. The evening was warm and clear. Derek Dell had a lifetime fascination with following the weather. It was important during his diving career and the habit persisted even after retirement. A calm night like this meant outdoor relaxation and the kind of family conversation excited visitors will have. Planning the next day's activities was highest on the list. Of course, Charlie was all set to begin his life as a free diver and scuba expert. Derek was certain of it!

Everyone seemed anxious for the snorkeling instruction to be first in the order of business. Charlie was already in the pool. He had no interest in planning but was more focused on doing. He would swim to the bottom and hold his breath as long as he could. "Did ya see, Poppy?" Charlie yelled with pride.

"Sure did, Charlie. When you swam toward the bottom of the pool, did your ears start to hurt a bit?" Dell asked.

"Yeah," Charlie replied. "A little bit."

"Don't worry about it, Charlie. I'll show you how to keep that from happening. It's all part of your training."

"Would you like to see my Zodiac?" Dell asked.

"What's a Zodiac?" Charlie queried.

"A Zodiac is an inflatable boat with a solid hull and floor," Dell replied. "Because they are tightly filled with air, they have a very shallow draft. That means they ride very shallow in the water."

"Are they rubber like the floats in the pool?" Charlie asked. "No, a Zodiac is made of a product called Hypalon. Hypalon is a multi-layered material that is tough as nails," Dell said with vigor. "it isn't bullet proof but Hypalon will take an extraordinary beating and keep on going.

"Zodiacs are used by advanced or military divers because of their light weight and extreme maneuverability. You can beach a Zodiac quite easily due to their buoyancy and they are unbelievable in the jungle," Dell stated.

"What's the jungle?" Charlie asked.

"Yeah, how does a boat work in the jungle? Aren't jungles on land?" added Drake.

Dell explained, "The jungle is the impact zone in the surf line. It is the most dangerous part of a wave because it's breaking or collapsing and tons of water are going in many directions. If you get caught inside and you find yourself in the jungle, a Zodiac is the boat you want. I've been surfing since I was six. I was taught to stay away from the jungle, even with a good surf board and leash. Since I have never been a very good surfer, I always heeded that advice and stayed clear of the jungle," Dell admitted. "C'mon, let's see the boat."

The sun was just dropping below the horizon. That burnt orange finality to a stunning day in paradise was a regular event at C-bay. A light by the water's edge illuminated the shallows on the beach in front of the house. As Darkness grew the light drew small fish of all kinds, stimulating a miniature feeding frenzy. Charlie, Drake and Derek walked past the light until they reached a palm tree.

A rope tied to the tree held the Zodiac safely in the near water. Hand over hand, Derek pulled the rope until the Zodiac began to slowly appear at the edge of the shoreline light. As the boat eased into the shallows Drake notice the boat's name painted on the bow. "*Maniac 4*," exclaimed Drake. "Since I know how you drive your sports cars back in California, I understand why you named your boat *Maniac*." Drake quipped. "My question is, what the hell happened to *Maniacs* 1, 2, and 3?" Drake asked.

"Well," moaned Dell, "it's a long story but I'm certain you already know the ending. That is, it was always my fault," laughed Dell. Derek's tone turned a bit more serious. "This boat is twenty feet, complete with high-end technology and comfort. It's the old man's version of Zodiac that suits me best these days. The previous *Maniacs* were only thirteen feet, stark and performance oriented.

"Very high-powered engines made them most effective in the jungle, too. There was never an unreachable dive site when we were in the *Maniacs* of old," Dell reminisced.

Back at the house Juliet was mixing mai tais. A touristy Polynesian drink, they are most refreshing and can pretty much guarantee a good night's sleep.

Lydia was in charge of the kitchen that evening. Rotation would guarantee a fine dining experience, given the number of skilled family cooks. Dinner was a light affair consisting of French cheeses, breads as a snack, various wines and a pasta primavera. Richly colored zucchini and bok choy were the featured vegetables. Every Italian dish prepared in the Dell kitchen required garlic, basil and an abundance of proper spices and herbs. Flavor was essential.

Everyone gathered around the large dining room table for their first home cooked meal in South Pacific. The emphasis is on the word "home". The first family dinner at C-bay was a milestone Juliet and Derek had dreamed of for years.

It was at that moment C-bay evolved from a vacation home to a family home. Derek thought he may have achieved the peaceful life he wanted so badly, ending his constant global trekking and high-risk activity.

Dinner was consumed leisurely. The excitement of arrival was giving way to the fatigue of travel. After a few goodnight kisses and hugs Juliet took Charlie's hand while Drake took Rachael's. Off they went to Tico's house next door. Juliet tucked Charlie in bed. All would sleep well.

Derek Dell was the son of a baker. Derek's Dad was up at three-thirty a.m. every day, keeping the early hours necessary for a baker. Young Derek was a light sleeper and his father's morning activities usually woke him by four a.m. Dad would put Derek to morning chores, mostly to keep him out of the way. Shoe-shining was Derek's most common contribution to the morning preparations. Here was reason for Dell's lifetime practice of arising at four a.m. These were the best hours of the day for Derek Dell. His mind was clear and rested. He did his best thinking during these moments.

Today was special. Though it had been some time since Derek Dell had taught beginners how to snorkel and free dive, today he would be particularly patient and thorough as the students were family.

Besides, Lydia would ensure nothing was overlooked with all safety measures fully in place. Derek Dell's diving career was not necessarily consistent with dive safety and observance of all the rules. Those days were surely over and safe sport diving had become Derek's rule, at least for the most part. Derek quietly made coffee, cooked an egg and added fruit to his morning fare.

Though still dark, Derek headed out for his daily run. Physical training was a permanent part of his life. As a younger man Dell was a catcher for the San Francisco Giants. His career as a baseball player was brief and injury-ridden. It left him with a lifelong need to remain fit. In the end, Dell felt, all those injuries were probably a good thing. Derek was a person who found an optimistic element to any situation.

By the time he finished his run Juliet was up and filled with energy. Juliet was a very serious grandmother. She felt that children were important people because of their youth and inexperience in life. Kids were society's renewable opportunity to fix itself.

If you nurtured them properly, thought Juliet, you have a chance to better the world. Most found that notion tough to disagree with. Juliet was a person who didn't just express a philosophy, she lived it.

The sun rose, coffee was sipped and the remainder of the family trickled into the kitchen at C-bay. Breakfast found its way to the table. Everyone did their own thing. Juliet ensured Charlie was stuffed with island eggs, fruit and French toast. She knew Charlie would be in the water all day long. She also knew that even eighty-five-degree water can break down your body heat and lead to dehydration and hypothermia. Thanks to Juliet's preparations Charlie would have fuel to burn so that could not occur.

The morning conversation was focused on relaxation and holiday fun. Nothing too serious was discussed beyond the weather conditions, water clarity and the likely creature encounters the snorkeling would provide.

The group adjourned to the beach. Charlie, on a dead run, was first to the assemblage of fins, masks and snorkels Derek had laid out. There was a proper size and fit for each diver. Dell ensured that the equipment his family used was of the highest quality for maximum enjoyment. Lydia had her own gear. She had been doing this since she was a little girl. "Lydia," Dell asked, "would you please show everyone how to properly fit the mask to their face? I forgot something at the house."

"Sure, Dad," Lydia replied. While Lydia

demonstrated how to seal the mask to prevent leaks, Derek dashed back to the house.

Quickly moving into the kitchen, he opened the freezer door and retrieved frozen green peas. Green Giant brand, it was. Returning to the group at high speed Derek noticed that Lydia had been a very effective teacher.

Charlie was eager to show Derek he could suck air through his nose and hold the mask to his face without using the strap. "That's the sign of a tight seal, Charlie. You're ready to go, buddy." Dell said. "Do your fins fit comfortably? You'll want to make sure they don't chafe or bind your feet. In a long outing that can be painful." Though the focus of the teaching was Charlie, Derek and Lydia were careful to ensure everyone understood the simple rules for safe snorkeling.

"Okay," Dell uttered. "We've covered the fins. Lydia showed you how to put on your mask. There's one more mask tip before we move on to the snorkel. As you dive heat and moisture from your face will cloud the inside of your mask. It may seem a bit gross but the best thing to do to prevent this is to spit in the mask. Rub it around a bit then rinse with salt water."

Lydia asked, "Dad, didn't you buy any mask clear?"

"No, sweetie," replied Dell. "We're teaching this part Fiji style." This was a term Dell often used when things were being done in a basic or old school manner. "You don't want to rely on mask clear to solve the problem. What if you lose your bottle? Run out? Divers need to know self-sufficiency and always have a Plan B." Small tidbits like this were the difference between sport divers and serious professionals.

Last was the snorkel. Dell explained, "You may think this simple piece of equipment is a mere breathing device. That's true. It is your access to air when your face is in the water. Also," Dell continued, "it is a resting device. The snorkel allows you to rest your head on the surface of the water while breathing comfortably. The more time your face is underwater, the more you will see and more you will enjoy." Everyone now had their face in the water and was adjusting to relaxed breathing through the snorkel. With the basic equipment sorted out, the group was now ready to learn how to move in the water and use the gear effectively.

"Dive gear of any kind is only designed to assist the diver. Enable a diver to maximize their God given physical abilities. The quality of the dive is always related to the quality of the diver and not quality of the gear." This was straight out of Derek Dell's long-held belief that physical fitness was an important part of military or professional diving.
Sport diving is the type of activity that unfit people can safely enjoy. Modern equipment and diving protocols provide an avenue where even disabled people can enjoy the ocean through the sport of scuba diving. On the other hand, fit divers are not only safer but are able to explore the ocean far more effectively.

Dell thought it important to launch Charlie into his ocean journey with the strong foundation and respect for fitness.

"Let's go over how to kick. The best way to propel yourself through the water is to remember one word. Smooth." Dell elongated the Os and slowly waved his hand in a level fashion. "The less resistance you offer the water, the less air and energy you use. Now, a snorkel gives you access to unlimited air so conservation is not so important. When you are diving with tanks air conservation is important, so learn to move smoothly through the water. Watch your kick. Don't pedal your legs like you were riding a bicycle, lock your knees and kick from the hip. Not only will this motion move you through the water more effectively, it will well tone the muscles in your legs and butt."

"All right!" yelled Rachael. "Does this mean I can give up my Brazil butt zumba class?"

Out of nowhere, Drake simply said, "No."

Derek observed his family of snorkelers and was duly impressed with Charlie's kick. This child was part dolphin! Young Charlie zoomed through the water.

Derek had thrown the bag of green peas on the beach near the water's edge. Everyone saw them but no comments were made. Finally, Charlie could wait no longer. "What are the peas for, Poppy?" he asked.

"Just wait, Charlie," Dell patiently said. "First, I want to show you how to actually go underwater with just a mask, snorkel and fins. Then we'll get to the peas."

"Okay, Poppy, diving under is the best part, huh?" asked Charlie.

"It sure is, Charlie. Floating on the surface is fun and there is always lots to see. But the best encounters come when you hold your breath, dive down and swim along the reef.

"Now, listen closely because this is really good to know. Before you dive down, I want you to take three giant breaths and blow them out. This clears out nitrogen in your lungs and makes more room for oxygen. Charlie, don't worry about the science, just remember the three big breaths. Recall how your ears began to hurt a bit in the pool last night?" Derek asked.

"Yes," said Charlie.

"That's because water is a lot thicker than air and when you go down pressure from the water pushes on your ear drums and hurts. The way to prevent that is to equalize. Before you ask, equalizing is making the pressure inside your ear drum equal to the pressure the water is putting on the outside of the drum. You probably experienced the same ear thing on the plane flying over, only to a lesser degree."

"I did, Poppy," said Charlie. "The flight attendant told me to chew and move my jaw around and it would clear up. Is that what I do snorkeling?" Charlie inquired.

"Not exactly," said Dell. "In water you have to

pinch your nose and gently try to exhale through your nose. Since it is pinched the pressure will back up through your ears and pop them, equal to the outside pressure. This takes a bit of practice and you should start equalizing before your face breaks under the water. Okay, everyone give it a try." Dell wandered through the shallow water watching each diver. Lydia did the same.

Though Juliet was a good diver she preferred to let Derek and Lydia handle the teaching. Charlie adapted to the training in a heartbeat. Able to clear his ears and easily equalize, he took his new-found skill to advanced levels right away. Each practice dive brought Charlie deeper and more comfortably curious. Even though the sandy bottom had been churned up by the practicing divers, limiting visibility, Charlie stayed under as long as his lungs allowed.

Everyone had their relative problems perfecting skills in equalizing. Drake, however, just could not get his ears to pop equal. Derek explained that often long periods of time on aircraft made it hard for some people to equalize. Perhaps in a day or so Drake's ears would adjust.

"As important as a proper descent is a proper ascent," Dell said. "When your lungs begin to tell you its's time to head up, ascend slowly, releasing air along the way. Never ascend faster than your bubbles. Raise your hand in a pointing motion toward the surface," Dell instructed.

"Why, Poppy?" asked Charlie.

"In case a boat is passing by or some other floating object, you will strike it with your hand rather than your head," Derek advised.

"When your head breaks the surface use a blast clear to empty your snorkel. The blast clear is simple. Just blow out through the snorkel as hard as you can. After a little practice you will be able to sufficiently empty the device. Your head need not ever leave the water nor your lips leave their seal."

The group practiced the techniques taught by Derek and all soon mastered the process except Drake. His ears continued to prevent descent. The others smoothly resumed relaxed breathing through their cleared snorkels.

"Now for the peas!" Dell proclaimed. "We're going to use an age-old trick for underwater photographers and animal trainers. FOOD," said Dell. "If you want to train a shark you have to use food as a control mechanism. The same is true of smaller fish as well. We just use smaller food. Make sense, Charlie?" asked Dell.

"I understand, Poppy. We're gonna feed peas to the fish so they will come close to us," Charlie said. With that, Derek and Lydia led the group out into the deeper waters of the bay.

Sandy bottom gave way to coral reef hosting an abundance of small sea life. Lydia was in front with Charlie and Juliet following, holding hands. Drake, Torchy and Rachael trailed closely behind. Derek floated around everywhere, making sure the divers were using proper mechanics: kicking from the hip; arms close to their sides; steady, relaxed breathing. These simple habits made even the first snorkel a far more enjoyable experience.

The dive site was only about seventy-five yards from the beach. Once the group reached the coral outcropping Dell opened the bag of peas. Everyone watched, curious as to the appetite fish had for green peas.

There was an explosion of activity. Even Lydia, who had seen this many times, was impressed with the reaction. She was certain her Dad had been working these fish regularly with the peas. No question, he was preparing the reef for his family Christmas snorkel trips. Charlie's eyes grew large inside his mask.

So many fish vied for the small peas that you couldn't see through the crowd. Eye-trembling color found in the various tropical species reminded all the divers of the Papeete market. Animal behavior was controlled by Dell's years of experience with feeding sea creatures of all sizes and types. The surface chatter and excitement of the family was exactly what Derek and Juliet had hoped for on their first family dive.

Derek staged the withdrawal of food from water and the activity slowed down. Rapid darting and frantic thrusting by various fish toward peas transformed into slow cruising with minimal interest in the divers. On the surface Dell asked, "Charlie, you wanna feed the fish?"

"Can I, Poppy?" Charlie pleaded.

"Sure you can. It's easy. Just release the peas from your hand, a few at a time. The more peas you release at once the more activity you will generate," Dell said.

Charlie quickly caught on. So did the fish. After a

while they seemed to line up, awaiting Charlie's next release. Behavior had been changed. It was only Charlie's first dive in the South Pacific and it seemed he had already made several new friends on the reef! All were thrilled.

As everyone swam back to shore after their snorkel it was clear they had experienced something which was quite unique. Gathered as a family at Christmas in the South Pacific simply had to begin its first day with a swim alongside friendly creatures most people will only see in aquariums.

Lobster Fantastico!

Once on the beach the divers realized they were more fatigued than they thought. The water has a way of silently robbing you of your energy. Add jet lag to the equation and a late morning nap seemed in order for the travelers. Derek and Juliet would prepare lunch.

The afternoon was warm. Too hot to be in the sun, or even outside for long. Perfect time to close the exterior doors, turn on air conditioning and set up the Christmas tree. "It is with great regret that I shamefully admit our Christmas tree is fake. Not the statuesque pines you remember from the many Christmases at Miracle Mountain Ranch but a plastic replica," Dell lamented, hanging his head. No one gave a damn. So went the entire afternoon. Not only was the tree well-groomed in island decor, a string of lights outlined the entire pathway from C-bay to Tico's place next door. Everyone participated in converting C-bay and Tico's into a Moorea Christmas destination. Neighbors were impressed, even the tourist drove out of their way to stop by. Most of all, the entire family created the event and had a great time doing so. In the end, Derek did not care about the plastic tree either. The evening cooled off and, as usual, all activity returned outdoors. With the Christmas lights in full bloom C-bay took on an enchanted atmosphere. Derek announced something special. "Tomorrow, Torchy, Juliet, Lydia and Rachael want to catch a morning ferry to Papeete. Do a little Christmas shopping, right?" asked Dell.

"Yes," replied the ladies in unison.

"While you are gone, Drake, Charlie and I will take the *Maniac* out and I'll do a special dive."

"What's a special dive, Poppy?" asked Charlie.

Juliet answered, "That's where Derek gets a load of lobsters and we barbecue a feast on the beach. With any luck he'll get enough to invite the neighbors."

This would be a spectacular event. Many of Juliet and Derek's neighbors were skilled in Tahitian dance, costume and culture. The opportunity for an extraordinary beach party was shaping up at C-bay. Very few Americans would ever see the South Pacific at a local level like this. Derek and Juliet were pleased.

That night Rachael and Torchy handled dinner. Rachael was a professional chef and Torchy took directions well. That meant another gourmet dinner at C-bay. The main course consisted of citrus salmon in mango pineapple salsa, sautéed rau-rau (Pacific spinach) in olive oil and garlic, and jasmine risotto. A variety of French wines was opened. No one drank to excess.

Tomorrow was to be a great time. Party plans were made while Derek pondered the best holes in the reef of his secret site in which to find lobsters. He checked the dive gear, ensuring his tanks were filled with nitrox (oxygen enriched air). Everyone retired happily, excited about the coming day.

The next morning Juliet couldn't wait to take the daughters to Papeete. Not only did this mean a manicure/pedicure, a great lunch and spirited conversation, it meant an opportunity to closely survey the Tahitian black pearl inventory of local jewelers. This would allow them to identify the specific pieces Drake and Derek would be directed to obtain as Christmas presents. Though this practice seems somewhat detached for a heartfelt Christmas present, it guarantees satisfaction. On a costly item like Tahitian black pearls you want the exact product. Everyone decided they could live with that. There was always the creativity of stocking stuffers for the thoughtful element of Christmas presents.

Derek, Charlie and Drake arrived early on the beach. Derek had already packed the *Maniac* with dive gear and drinks. He fired the twin forty-five Yamahas, released the bow line and turned the idling *Maniac* toward a distant reef.

As soon as Derek had cleared the inner waters, he bumped the *Maniac* to full throttle. On a quick plane they reached the dive site in no time. Derek was certain his secret lobster heaven would provide the bounty needed for his holiday table. He assembled his dive gear with confidence and the obvious experience of a long-term pro. The dive gear used by Dell seemed more a natural part of his body than an "add-on".

"Okay," said Derek. "Here's how the system works. Drake, put a line over the side. When I fill this game bag with lobster I'll swim over, hook it to the line and tug three times. That'll signal you to haul it up. Charlie, you can snorkel around the boat and watch me from above. I will be at fifty feet. That's probably deeper than you can free dive but why not take a shot?" Derek suggested. "If I'm lucky, the entire dive will not exceed thirty minutes."

Over the side Dell plunged. Quickly adjusting, his descent was rapid and direct. He knew exactly where he was going. Dell settled on the reef's outer wall in about fifty-five feet of water.

The first two lobsters were easy. He didn't even use the Hawaiian bola spear he carried. A snatch-and-grab technique worked just fine. Derek Dell was not a prolific hunter but he was doing very well on this dive. His confidence soared and he envisioned his telephone call inviting the neighbors. This was actually pretty easy. He caught the lobsters while they were drowsy and was willing to bend a few local laws to get the main course he needed. This was going to be a memorable beach party.

Finally, he was presented with a challenge. While moving down the reef Dell came upon a crevice where at least six bugs, as divers called lobster, were sitting. Derek couldn't see their bodies but the feeler tentacles were sticking out. Nearly half Dell's body slid into the crevice. Slowly he approached the prey, easing and twisting himself further into the crack. He thought he could spear two, perhaps three on one shot if he slipped close enough. Dell gradually extended his arm to release the spear.

As his arm reached full length, he felt a paralyzing pain emanating from his wrist. Following the pain was an enormous blood gush coming from the hit. Whatever attacked Derek Dell was not letting go and was far stronger than him. Dell struggled to get free. Of more concern was the rate at which he was consuming air. He was only diving with a pony tank. This had to be an eel, Dell thought. In this area it just had to be. Probably spotted white-mouth moray. They get huge. The eel released its clamp but then bit again, sending Dell to the doorstep of panic.

The situation only got worse. A disturbance of this degree in otherwise calm morning moments sends action signals everywhere on the reef. Dell had often seen sea snakes in this area. He also saw them in the crevice, repeatedly pecking at the thin skin torn by the gripping jaws of the eel. Dell knew each nibble sent poison into his blood stream. Repeated bites by multiple animals would pump enough juice into Dell to kill him. Unlikely, however, because paralysis would soon cause the regulator to fall from Dell's mouth. He would surely drown before the venom took his life.

Derek slipped further away from logic, focus and clear thinking. He was overwhelmed by pain and beginning to feel the toxic effects of the sea snake attacks. The eel was strong and relentless, not letting go. Dell was losing blood.

Everyone who lives on this earth will one day die. Intellectually we accept this quite readily. He didn't like to think about it or ever ponder the process but Derek Dell knew one thing about life. Nobody gets out alive.

His career was filled with high-risk diving and he had come to terms with death years ago. The older people get, the more comfortable they become with their mortality. It seemed that everyone from Mother Nature to Father Time had tried to kill Derek over the years. Today, it appeared sea snakes were going to finally complete the job. There is a point where we all surrender.

As Dell approached his end the events of his life began to flash before his eyes. He tumbled through his childhood, catching glimpses of his mother, father and older brother Wesley. His family house in San Francisco became a family house in Burlingame. The little league baseball games he played became major league ball with the San Francisco Giants.

Baseball was Derek's first level of accomplishment. It was no surprise that, in the final moments preceding death, he would relive the events of that time.

Bat, Ball and Beyond

Dell's mind flashed to 1972. Derek was graduating from college. His academic efforts had always been of minimal interest to him as he had attended school on a baseball scholarship and was headed to the majors. Dell was six feet two and two hundred thirty-five pounds. He was lean but muscular. A lifetime of weight training salted with steroid abuse had made him strong and very fast. These were the desirable traits in a major league catcher. Added to the fact he could hit the ball a mile, Derek was poised for a long career of big-league ball.

Two important skills necessary to a major-league catcher were an ability to make a swift and accurate throw to second base, picking off runners, and the ability to guard home plate when a runner tried to beat the ball home. Derek developed a profound ability at both. If you tried to make that play at home plate, Derek Dell was certain to hit you like a freight train. At times it seemed he was not interested in actually catching the ball and tagging the runner out. He would fully concentrate on delivering the most severe blow possible to any runner invading his space. This scared the hell out of the opposing players.

It was baseball that made Derek special

throughout his entire childhood and young adult years. Life was easy for a baseball star. You are treated well, looked after and all you have to do is play baseball better than the next guy.

Growing up in this vacuum gave many high-end athletes unrealistic views of the world and a detachment from everyday realities. Such was the case with Derek Dell. The amount of life experience Derek didn't have would fill volumes. The shelter of baseball made Derek Dell a very late bloomer.

Dreams were coming true. Derek entered the Giants' training facility in Arizona. His reputation for home plate collisions preceded his arrival. Dell had never in his life had a very serious thought about anything but baseball. He had played many sports as a young man but baseball was the focus.

Now was his chance to demonstrate the result of a lifetime of commitment, training and practice. Coaches liked his speed and batting skills. They decided to give him time in a preseason game against the Dodgers. Even though this was only a practice or exhibition game, it was the Dodgers. The rivalry between the two clubs has existed since they migrated from New York. Of personal importance to Derek was the fact the game was televised. This would be a showcase!

By the third inning Derek had grounded out and hit a double. He was pleased. Now, with Dell behind the plate, the heart of the Dodger lineup was coming to bat. Dell's mind flashed rapidly. He saw hit after hit. Bases were loaded. The next batter hit an infield grounder. The stage was set for Derek to highlight his key skill, guarding home plate.

The Giants were all great players. Derek knew the ball would be quickly scooped by the short stop and fired to Derek for the home plate play. This would happen with more speed than Derek had ever encountered in baseball. The pro game is always about speed. Speed of the pro players also meant the Dodger runner coming from third base would arrive at home plate faster than Derek had ever encountered in baseball.

The ball flew from the hand of the short stop. The runner charged home plate. Derek positioned himself for the collision of a career! Everyone was waiting for this moment. Players, coaches, fans, everyone. Derek was going to give them what they wanted. The problem was, the Dodger base runner felt the same way.

Merely the sound of the impact caused an eerie quiet in the ball park. Both benches emptied. Angry baseball players were converted into angry street fighters. Derek was ejected from the game.

Dell's mind flashed through the sounds, visions and pain of other baseball games as he struggled to retain life in Cook's Bay. He flashed on being ejected from other games though, in the throes of dying, he did not focus on detail of why, where or when.

He flashed to the moment he was ejected from baseball entirely. Even while fighting to hold on to consciousness, the depression of Dell's exit from baseball decades ago overwhelmed even the fear of imminent death by drowning.

He left baseball with numerous injuries. Six knee operations, shoulder dislocations and broken bones everywhere. Most irritating was his fractured neck. It left him with a lifetime habit of snapping his neck into place with a quick head jerk. The crackling sound made people uncomfortable.

He flashed on the dark time that followed baseball. Taken from him was the lifelong label of "special". Gone were the perks and status of being an elite athlete. The pathway to emotional recovery from this dreadful shock was completely unknown to Derek. The only thing Dell knew for certain was that he was finished with baseball and not on good terms.

Paralysis from the sea snake bites was beginning to inhibit Dell's breathing. He experienced momentary focus and clarity. During these brief episodes Dell fought to free himself from the crevice and the jaws of the white-mouth eel. Quickly though, the snake venom would regain its hold and Dell became motionless.

His mind tumbled through the 1970s rapidly covering the years after baseball. Derek pursued his lifelong passion for sports cars by racing. Though he loved the speed and excitement, it did not satisfy his career needs and was an unrealistic profession. Derek Dell was simply too big a guy to effectively race sports cars. Other types of racing involved larger cars but

Dell was only interested in the road-racing aspect of sports cars.

Life moved on. Derek had some money so he attended law school at night while working during the day for an insurance company, legal staff. His life wandered. So did the flashes as he lay underwater in Cook's Bay. The one constant was his repeated flash on surfing and diving. Scuba diving became Derek Dell's principle sport for both pleasure and rehabilitation from his various orthopedic injuries.

He flashed on suits, ties and downtown San Francisco. Dell finally settled on a career path in the reinsurance business. CCC Re was born. Triple C Re, as it was called, stood for Cost Contained Concepts Reinsurance. Reinsurers generally insure insurance companies. Reinsurance appealed to Derek Dell because he could use his legal training, play on his minor celebrity and easily do this kind of work his entire life. Since he did not feel the business was very challenging there was ample time for him to pursue his growing passion for scuba diving. The 70s would conclude in a positive feeling.

Dell somehow felt emotional comfort as he began to slip further toward unconsciousness in Cook's Bay.

Out on the Town!

Dell flashes to the 1980s. A house in Moss Beach, a marriage and a growing career shoot passed in the flicker of a brain synapse. He continues to develop dive skills and becomes a published underwater photographer. The "special" he lost when baseball ended accidentally returned through his growing portfolio of dramatic underwater photographs.

The need to create art through his images was an increasing desire. Dell never expected life to go in these two directions. The reinsurance business seemed very normal and comforting. He ran it with pride. Dell liked normal. There is great security in the herd, he thought. At the same time, traveling the world as an underwater photographer became a profession. There was certainly nothing normal about that job. The steady hand of a traditional reinsurance business, added to the adventure of an underwater photography career, provided the balance of life so necessary to Derek Dell.

Fall of 1981. Dell is in his blue and yellow Dodge van headed to a sport diving day boat in Monterey, Ca. Photographers from all over the world come to Monterey Bay to capture images of bountiful sea life in the area. Derek is lucky. Monterey is only a two-hour drive from his Moss Beach home. Since both Moss Beach and Monterey are on the ocean, the drive down California's Highway 1 takes you past some of the most beautiful coastline in the world. The panoramic visions never got old.

He loads his dive and photo gear onto the boat. It is early and cold. The boat dives twenty. Everyone on board is sipping tea or coffee. Cold water diving is demanding. The kelp beds of Monterey Bay can be a little tricky as well. The safety factor of a good dive buddy counts highly in this type of diving. Derek Dell didn't have one.

The captain announces they have arrived at the dive site. "Gear up and buddy up," is announced. Solo diving is not allowed. You must find a dive buddy or join another pair. This day, sitting alone on the gunnel was a single diver like Dell. "Good morning, are you solo?" asked Dell.

"Sure am," replied the dressing diver.

"My name is Derek Dell. Wanna buddy up?" Dell inquired."

"Let's do it. My name is Arthur Townsend," said the diver.

"Very pleased to meet you," said Dell.

"Likewise," said Arthur Townsend.

As they shook hands Derek could not help but be impressed with the power of Townsend's grip. They were an unlikely pair. Townsend was an intellectual, finance and investment professional. His vocabulary and demeanor reflected solid background and education. Townsend was not physically impressive. Dell would keep an eye on the safety situation. The conditions, though cold, were calm and the visibility underwater was expected to be fifty feet. That is fantastic for Monterey Bay.

They entered the water. The skill level of a scuba diver is often evident in the first four minutes of the dive. Dell eyed Townsend's adjustments and acclimation protocols. Buoyancy, face mask and ear clearing, the works. Dell observed every aspect of Townsend's entry system. As it happened, Townsend was doing exactly the same thing to Dell. The mutual inspection was important. After all, their safety was dependent upon one another.

The two strangers moved through the water effortlessly. Dell was impressed with Townsend's clearly advanced diving skills. It was evident from the look in Townsend's eye that he thought the same of Dell.

The divers surfaced an hour or so later. Because of good navigational utilities they surfaced directly by the boat ladder. "Wow!" exclaimed Dell. "You dive like a harbor seal. Very impressive, Mr. Townsend, very impressive," Dell repeated.

The ocean is a great equalizer. Though Derek was keen on fitness, strength and size do not matter underwater. The sea is bigger and stronger than any of us. What is important is the diver's understanding of the conditions, hydrodynamics and their equipment. It was clear that these two divers were capable on any aspect of the sport. Mutual confidence was growing. Trust in your dive buddy changes the nature of your dive. Less concern over your buddy and more concentration on photo work will produce better artwork, Dell thought. Day boat diving in Monterey usually includes two dives. The second dive left Dell even more impressed with Townsend than the first. After the boat returned to the harbor Dell asked Townsend to join him in a needed bowl of hot clam chowder. Perhaps a beer or two would go down well.

The divers adjourned to a dockside venue where the friendship blossomed. Though cold and tired, the two spent hours getting to know one another. Dell confessed, "Ya know, the only reason I was on that boat was to identify all the best dive sites. The truth is, I have a Zodiac."

Townsend ceased sipping the soup, his eyes raised from the bowl to meet Dell's. A potato fell from his spoon. Townsend knew that Zodiacs were both the best piece of dive gear one could have and, at the same time, very dangerous items indeed. Due to a Zodiac's poor distribution of weight, they tend to flip over backwards. Though extremely lightweight and buoyant, the heavy engine on the rear of the boat threw the balance way off. Also, because they are filled with air, at high speed they can actually bounce like a beach ball and overturn. Derek drove everything at high speed.

It is one matter for Arthur Townsend to trust a stranger like Derek for a sport dive off a Monterey boat, it is quite another to head out to sea with him in a Zodiac. For all the advantages a Zodiac provides, they come with risk too. For that reason, Zodiacs were normally reserved for use by pros.

The day ended late. Derek had grown to respect Arthur in a number of ways. They planned more dives, shook hands again and began the drive, up Highway 1. Townsend lived in San Francisco so his drive was a half hour more than Dell's.

Triple C Re was doing well. Derek had put staff in charge while he took a lesser role. This allowed him to concentrate on his underwater photo work. The week after Arthur and Derek's meeting was used to organize their dive trip planned for the next weekend. All photo gear was ready to go, dive gear sorted and, above all, the Zodiac was thoroughly performance-ready.

They would be camping out and launching the Zodiac from the beach nearest the dive sites. Dell had freedom of time. That meant he would leave on Thursday in order to secure a good site at the local camp ground. Arthur Townsend would arrive late Friday night. The camp fire was burning.

The blue van was amazing. Fitted with a bed, sink, stove and small TV it was the ideal vehicle from which to headquarter a dive trip. The van could go anywhere and tow the Zodiac with ease.

That night Arthur arrived about seven-thirty. Dell had prepared a vegetable and fish soup and the two settled in. The conversation was excited.

They planned two dives, the Zodiac launch point and all logistics for a safe but intensive cold-water dive.

Technical structure was vital. The two divers exchanged ideas and opinions. Dell could see Arthur had impressive knowledge of the tidal and current conditions, subaquatic terrain and expected animal life.

Dell noted that Arthur shared his opinion on adrenalin junkie vs adventurer. There was a vital distinction. Simple thrill seekers view a given event as an opportunity to snap those adrenal glands open and feel the rush! Adventurers like Derek and Arthur view their activity differently. Certainly, there is a blast of excitement but the foundation of structure is grounded in curiosity and pursuit of knowledge. In the end they settled on the basic notion that if there was no "maybe" there was no fun.

An impressive exchange of planning skills ended with both divers more confident in the other. The conversation turned social. "Arthur, I have always enjoyed camp fire chats. Folks are generally relaxed and conversation opens easily. For me, it's the sort of night on the town I prefer these days," Dell confessed. Arthur agreed.

"I saw you play baseball once," said Arthur out of nowhere. "It was a great game, only, as I recall, you were ejected." Arthur smiled.

Dell sheepishly replied, "It is possible that I may have, on occasion, approached the game with excessive exuberance," like he was reading a prepared statement for the press.

On advice of counsel Dell made such formal statements until all of the Statutes of Limitation had run out on his conduct during baseball. "Surprised as hell you remember a nobody baseball player like me."

"Well," said Town, "I probably wouldn't if it weren't for the ejections. Didn't you set a major league record for those?"

As the evening progressed the conversation wandered in all directions. This is how people should communicate. The sincerity one must present when planning dangerous activity brings out more sincerity when other matters of life are discussed. It was becoming clear that Arthur was literally the smartest person Dell had ever met. There was no question in Derek's mind that he would enjoy many dive/photo trips with Arthur Townsend. That meant a nickname must be selected. From that night on Arthur Townsend would simply be "Town" to Derek Dell.

The next morning both divers rose early. The convenience of the van was helpful during pre-dive protocols. A quick breakfast was important. It would help the body deal with the cold Monterey waters.

The beach launch was a snap. Town and Dell worked out both entry and exit strategies on the perfect beach location. Conditions were favorable. The Zodiac performed flawlessly. Dell began to test the limits of the boat, ensuring he could navigate to safety if the sea turned ugly. Town moved to balance the boat, minimizing the weight distribution problems inherent in Zodiacs. Town needed no direction. As Dell drove more aggressively, Town instinctively found the exact sweet spot on the boat from which to achieve the safest balance.

Both divers geared up and did back-roll water entries off the Zodiac pontoons. It seemed as though they had been diving together for years.

The Monterey underwater ecosystem is one of the most vibrant on planet Earth. Hundreds of square miles were declared a marine reserve in the early 1970s. A decade later the environment was thriving.

Water temperature was only mid-fifties. Dell and Town were wearing thick wet suits, full hoods and heavy gloves. All that rubber meant a bunch of lead on the weight belt too. Cold water diving is a heavy lift. In the water, however, the two divers quickly achieved a state of neutral buoyancy. This state of weightlessness permitted Dell to steadily compose photographs to achieve maximum artistic output from each dive.

Film limitations of those days required careful planning. Overcast conditions combined with calm seas meant minimal plankton bloom to cloud visibility. This allowed Derek to use a wide-angle lens to capture the cathedral-like nature of a kelp forest. Fish were plentiful.

Town broke open an urchin, creating a miniature feeding frenzy directly in front of Derek's Nikon. That activity brought the pinnipeds. Seals and otters were the prominent pinnipeds in the area. They had flourished after the Marine Mammal Act passed in the

70s. Seals shot up to the mask of each diver. After barking out air bubbles to announce their presence the seals raced off to perform acrobatics. They were a playful end to the first dive of the day. Derek left the water with a camera full of money shots.

Birth of the Maniac

It is 1983. Dell and Town had been diving together for a couple of years. They begin to travel the world diving some of the most exotic locations on earth. The Caribbean, South China Sea, the South Pacific were all amongst their treks. The Northern California coast remained their primary dive area. After all, that was home.

Along the way Town acquired a good bit of underwater photo gear. Of course, he became an excellent nature photographer as well. His animal knowledge and grasp of science provided him with the perfect background to create stunning images. Town was obviously talented.

Both divers bought dry suits. All that cold-water diving using only a wet suit was getting too uncomfortable. A wet suit allows water to seep in. That water is heated by the body and warmth is sustained for a period of time. A dry suit is quite different. No water enters the suit at all. They are well engineered to prevent leakage. The divers wore warm full body snow gear under the outer layer of the suit. Dry suits also fill with air. This keeps the ocean cold away from the body, protecting it with a layer of air. The tricky part comes from the buoyancy challenges arising from pumping air into the suit. It's an adjustment for sure. Well worth it for the comfort. Town and Dell made the dry suit adjustments quickly and safely.

As their dive skills soared, so did the level of risk they assumed. Moreover, Derek spent endless time in the Zodiac training in various conditions. His confidence and abilities with the craft were now at a high level that Dell never expected. He later confessed that his Zodiac talents stemmed from his experience as a surfer.

Dell believed surfing was, in essence, riding the rhythm of the earth. Understanding that everything from the heartbeat of a baby to the changing of the tides is an earthly rhythm. Surfing permits you to join the rhythm of the ocean as it generates sets of waves. His background as a surfer, added to the Zodiacs's torque prop and powerful engine, opened up any dive site under any conditions to Town and Dell.

Dell had scored a challenging underwater photo assignment. It seems there was talk of opening up Northern California to offshore oil drilling. The controversy was unimaginable. Derek had mixed emotions because he and Town had dived the Channel Islands near Santa Barbara on many occasions. The oil rigs there had actually become artificial reefs. Housing numerous forms of sea life, these metal platforms provided the electrolysis that sparked reef growth. Conversely, an oil spill in a Marine Reserve could be devastating. Dell took the compensatory position and set out with Town to do the job.

They would be diving off the coast of Big Sur. Their launch point was a spot called Julia Pfeiffer State Beach. This area did not have enough hotels or support systems to accommodate a pro photo gig like this. Town and Dell would be camping out and totally self-sufficient. There was no place to fill tanks, no boat launch ramps or other niceties. Of even more concern, the location was at the edge of the Great Pacific Trench. This giant underwater canyon was the domain of the great white shark.

It was agreed that Town would act as a safety observer and Dell would shoot the film. This strategy allowed Town to bring a spear and hunt dinner. Before they could even begin to worry about great white sharks or dinner the divers had to figure out a way to get the Zodiac in the water.

The waves were huge! California waves are thick and powerful. When a strong swell moves over the Pacific Trench it grows the wave in height. Such were the conditions this day. Any dive team would abort. There was simply no way a flipover-prone Zodiac filled with exotic dive and photo gear could possibly survive the breakers. Town and Dell were certain to end up in the jungle, fighting for survival and the next breath of air. On the other hand, the two had such overwhelming confidence in one another they actually believed they could make it. This was the recipe for a big mistake.

The two dragged the boat and all the gear to the

water's edge. At this point a crowd began to assemble. People were surprised that the divers were even contemplating a launch. Dell paced back and forth, eyeing each set of waves. More people joined the spectators. One of the audience was a photographer for the *Sacramento Bee*. She began shooting the event in detail.

Down the beach strolled Town's girlfriend Melissa. She had driven down from San Francisco to help the divers with logistics. Melissa was wide-eyed as she saw the boys pacing up and down the beach. Surely they were not going to launch, she thought.

The final decision was Dell's. He was the surfer, the Zodiac pilot. Town had grown to trust his dive buddy implicitly. Whatever call Dell made, Town would follow.

The crowd continued to swell. No one knew who Melissa was, so they spoke openly about the pending disaster and "those two idiots". Odds of making it through the surf line were discussed by the watchers. Soon, bets were made and money changed hands.

Dell and Town continued their evaluation of the conditions. The waves were building and prospects for the launch were worsening. If they were going to do it, it had to be now.

Just off center at Julia Pfeiffer was an outcropping of rock extending about twenty-five feet in the air. The water behind the rock is sheltered from the waves, shallow and less turbid. This was where the Zodiac's minimal draft offered a glimmer of hope for a launch.

Dell and Town eased the bow into the water. Over half the boat remained on the sand.

They packed the dive gear tightly in the bow. Tanks, weight belts, cameras and anything heavy was roped in forward. Their hope was to offset the flipping tendencies of the boat with heavy metal from the gear.

Once the boat was ready Town and Dell zipped up their dry suits and pushed the remainder of the Zodiac into the shallow calm behind the rock.

Now there were more cameras clicking away in the crowd onshore. Where in hell did all these people come from? thought Dell. This only added stress to the situation.

The strategy was to hide in safety behind the rock until the precise moment in the wave set arrived. Derek would then hit the juice. Town offered one last glance at Dell to assure him of conviction and commitment. Dell returned a glare of focus and confidence. The onlookers backed away and grew even more astonished at what they were about to witness.

Town was stationed at the front of the Zodiac. Dell was still standing in the shallow water, controlling the craft until the engine fired. One pull and the power plant was alive. He remained in the water, carefully staring at the waves, looking for the right opportunity. Afraid of the bounce factor associated with Zodiacs, Dell jumped on the boat, grabbed the bow line and leashed it to his left wrist. With the engine tiller in his right hand, Derek could assume a squatting, surfing position to handle the bounce they would certainly encounter. Town was on his knees grabbing pontoon rope to accomplish the same, only remaining low enough for Dell to see over him. The proper moment had come.

Dell hit the gas for everything the Zodiac was worth. The torque prop kicked in and the forward thrust amazed. The weight distribution system worked well and the Zodiac planed instantly. The boat literally screamed around the corner from behind the rock. It achieved full speed in an instant. A hard right turn caused the rear end to fishtail a bit. Now the divers were headed directly at the wave set, hoping to pass into to the open sea.

The waves were about fifteen feet on the face. Thick and powerful, there was no way the Zodiac could punch through the wave, it had to go over the top. If they did not clear the top before the wave pitched, the Zodiac would surely flip backwards, depositing the divers in the jungle, the impact zone of the wave.

The high whine of the engine built as they neared the face. The Zodiac arched when the base of the wave was encountered. It seemed to pick up speed as the small boat climbed the face. More than halfway up both Town and Dell felt they would not make it. Derek sensed the pitch coming and they were not far enough up the face to clear the top. Both men instinctively moved forward.

The next thing they knew, the Zodiac was high in the air. With no resistance from water the engine whine grew to an explosive level. Both divers leaned further forward, Dell using the bow line and his stance to balance both the boat and himself. The bright red craft shot into the air, powered by the engine and the thrust of the California trench born wave.

The flight was level and controlled. The descent was the same. Shock came when the boat finally hit the water on the other side of the wave. The engine revolutions had grown so high during the boat's air-time that when it hit the water it took off like a rocket, straight out to sea. The elation that followed was only surpassed by their absolute confusion at the fact that they had made it.

Back on the beach the assembled crowd burst into applause, yelling and whistling. Wave piercing like this was simply never seen before. Dell and Town, wanting to put up a good front for the audience, acted as though they did such things every day. They never let their terror of the moment show. Someone in the group asked, "Who are those maniacs?" Melissa lowered her stance to assume anonymity and provided no answer. She did, however, make friends with the newspaper photographer and later produced a photo documentary of the event.

There was little question that this was the day the *Maniac* was born. It was unclear whether the *Maniac* was the Zodiac or Derek himself. Derek settled the matter by naming the boat and painting *Maniac* on the bow.

For the next decade and a half Dell and Town rode and flew the *Maniac* to dive sites all over Northern California. The Mendocino coast, Sonoma County coast, Sea Ranch, Gerstle Cove, Monterey, all the sites that offered opportunity for the friends to photograph and dive California's abundant biosystems.

They would often be joined by others. Their buddies would connect with the divers at the camp sites to enjoy abalone or speared cod harvested by Town. These were memorable times for everyone.

After each dive they would take the *Maniac* for a wild ride. Dell's surfing experience and wave-reading ability provided for adrenalin-soaked post-dive thrills. Piloting the *Maniac* in this fashion was a unique skill which complemented Derek's surfing and diving passions very well. Things only got better, but more dangerous.

Enter the Shark

In 1983 Derek became interested in sharks. Dell seemed haunted by a drive that forced him to do everything to an extreme. As a diver and nature photographer there was no more example of "extreme" than sharks.

At that time there was no real body of knowledge about sharks. Derek ventured from his Moss Beach home to the Half Moon Bay City Library. There was little in the way of information except a book penned in 1963 by an unknown author plainly named John Brown. Repeatedly the book told of the far-off archipelago of Rangiroa. Technically it was French Polynesia. Realistically, it may as well have been located on Mars.

Rangiroa housed a large lagoon. The tidal action of each day forced thousands of tons of water through a passage at one end. This was the Avatoro Pass. The Pass was an underwater canyon connecting the warm shallow waters of the inner lagoon to the deep blue abyss of the great Pacific. The speed and pressure of the water exiting the lagoon and dumping into the deep was dangerous. Too dangerous to dive much of the time.

If you survived the high-speed wash out of the

lagoon you would be faced with a variety of sharks who feed heartily on the Pass's deposited sea life. The sharks saw the Pass as easy pickings twice a day. Added to the big wave surface break (a surfer's dream) the Avatoro Pass could easily be one of the most perilous places on earth. So many scenarios existed for serious trouble, Derek could not even form a strategy for photographing the animals.

Curiosity and challenge soon turned into opportunity. The word was out. Actor Marlon Brando was planning to sell his private island of Tetiaora. It was also located in French Polynesia. The eccentric star wanted some underwater video of sharks. It was to be part of a production featuring his island home. Derek wanted his hat in the ring for that gig. He knew he could get what Brando wanted if he went to Rangiroa. This could be a huge career move. A Marlon Brando job would look pretty good in Dell's resume. He set out for Rangiroa and the Avatoro Pass.

Dell arrived in Tahiti exhausted from the crippling process of getting his battery of dive and photo gear that far away. Everything was metal, heavy yet fragile. Camera housings could be rendered useless by the bend of a single handle or adjustment shaft. Moreover, technical diving in faraway destinations required that you bring two of everything. Loss of any critical gear could terminate the shoot before it ever got started. Not to mention the vexatious nature of film. One errant pass through an airport X-ray machine could wipe out the product of an entire expedition. It was indeed a production.

Dell decided two days in Papeete booked at the Sheraton were in order. From there he could detail the intricate ordeal of getting to Rangiroa. French Polynesia was Dell's preferred island paradise. Paris seemed to have things pretty well under control and logistics were manageable. Both Derek and his equipment landed safely in Rangaroa three days later.

Dell immediately booked his hotel and set out to find a scuba operator who could handle the incredible difficulties of a drift dive through the Avatoro Pass.

As it turned out the crack team of dive professionals secured by Dell for this purpose were a French barman named Christophe who was, well, drunk much of the time, and a village boatman who occasionally fished in the area. Dell was certain the air in the tanks would stink of stale beer and that the boat would likely run out of gas halfway out. Off they went to, oh yes, One of the most perilous places on earth.

Another problem existed. None of the three men on the shabby wooden boat spoke the same language. Christophe spoke only French. Occasionally he could belch up an English word or two but certainly not if he was excited or pressured. Under stress even his French speech began to slur.

Dell, at first, thought Christophe might be a stroke survivor. Later he learned Christophe was merely drunk on a regular basis. As for the boatman,

Dell was never even able to determine the man's name, let alone what local language he might speak.

Bursting with confidence, Derek set out to sea with his two new friends. The dive strategy, as communicated by grunts and hand signals, was pretty simple. It would certainly be a drift dive. They would enter the water in the shallow calm of the lagoon. Christophe would act as safety diver.

A large bright orange buoy was cast over board. Gilles followed, grabbing the buoy tether rope. The unknown boatman handed Gilles a speargun. Derek observed Christophe' protocols and comfort level. Christophe seemed to have good skills. Dell entered the water and made the needed camera adjustments, given light and conditions.

As the two descended to the sandy bottom Christophe eyed a small grouper. He cocked the speargun and instantly fired. To Dell's surprise, Christophe hit the fish dead center in the gills. Pretty good for a guy who likely could not pass a blood alcohol test.

Soon the white-tip and black-tip sharks appeared. These animals tend to pack hunt in the evening or early morning but the struggling of the grouper, added to the blood in the water, drew their curiosity.

Dell's camera lit up. The two swam toward the Pass. Dell could feel the current picking up. Christophe floated above, hanging onto the buoy and controlling the grouper. The boat followed the buoy.

Dell dropped down deeper and deeper. As they

approached the Pass Christophe ditched the grouper. There was enough blood in the current line to put the big guys outside the Pass on notice. The white-tips devoured the grouper in an instant. Dell dropped lower until he reached a depth of one hundred, twenty feet. The current speed increased dramatically.

Through the Pass they shot. Derek was moving so swiftly he could not compose a picture. As he exited the Pass his depth reached a maximum of one hundred, sixty feet. It was unnecessary for him to dive that deep but there was a photographic motive in play.

Dell wanted mouth shots. The best way to photograph those animals is to slowly swim up from the deep, shooting upward on the passing sharks. The slight up angle allowed strobe lighting to fill the underside of the shark, where the mouth is found.

This was working. Dell remained close to the wall so at least one side of his body was unapproachable. He could see the silhouette of Christophe about a one hundred, twenty feet above him. Christophe had steadied the buoy directly over Dell's bubble trail.

Dell used Nikon F3-T cameras in Oceanic Hydro 35 housings. Ikelite strobes. It was high-end pro gear but the manual nature of the cameras demanded continuous attention. Dell frequently stopped along the way to make camera adjustments. He did not see a tiger shark which was approaching from below.

Humans are not part of the tiger shark's normal prey. The blood in the water from the grouper was doing its job. The blood was insufficient to cause a frenzy but enough to cause curiosity.

Tiger sharks satisfy their curiosity by taking a

"test bite". The problem for Dell was that a test bite from a ten-foot apex predator is probably fatal.

Most divers, over time, will have casual contact with sharks. Ordinarily the sharks will turn tail and flee. The game changes substantially when you introduce feeding signals. The tiger undulated slowly toward Derek from beneath. Somewhat startled, Dell looked away from the camera and discovered the animal when it was only about ten feet away.

In order to satisfy the tiger's curiosity without suffering a test bite Dell quickly searched his mind for an answer. He decided that the regulator bubbles generated by hitting the purge button would create confusing vibration. The tiger veered off before Dell could remove the regulator from his mouth.

All added up, the dive was a great success. Dell had learned at least one element to safe shark-wrangling was to control the food cautiously. Finding the sweet spot between curiosity and frenzy was vital.

For the next ten days Dell, Christophe and No-Name continued diving the Pass. Tiger sharks, grey reef sharks, nurse sharks and even great hammerhead sharks, all swam the waters outside the Avatoro Pass. Near the end Derek abandoned the cameras and concentrated on studying animal behavior, reaction to different stimulus and feeding techniques.

No one knew, at the time, how Dell's Rangiroa visit would change the lives of so many divers from all over the world. Divers like Christophe are part of a great unknown group of pioneers. They are the original shark wranglers: people of adventure who one day entered the ocean, determined to discover how to dive with the deadliest creatures on earth. They had no idea what they were doing but went ahead and did it anyway. They used no cages or bang sticks. They gently supplied food stimulation and sought safety only in their trust in the sharks. The originals were gone or retired before *Shark Week* on Discovery Channel made celebrities of such folks. That's okay, they never did it for fame or fortune. Hats off to all pioneers.

Dell headed back to California having learned valuable shark-wrangling lessons. As for actor Marlon Brando, he decided not to sell his island after all. Even so, this had been a great trip.

Tubbataha, the End of Innocence

Dell's mind flashed to spring of 1984. After returning from Rangiroa he received a call from Town. They set a lunch date in the financial district of San Francisco. Town showed up in a fine Brooks Brothers suit, gold-rimmed glasses and white shirt. He did not appear to be the high adventure guy he actually was. He looked more like the investment banker type. With controlled enthusiasm Town explained that his new girlfriend (and later wife) had connections in the Philippines.

Few locations in the world offered the variety of sea life found in the South China Sea. There was a further lure. Since the end of the Viet Nam War, heroin trafficking had become prevalent in South East Asia. From the fabled Golden Triangle flowed opium, necessary to process the end product, to waiting Chinese junks off the coast of Viet Nam.

The junks sailed for Hong Kong Harbor under the guise of fishing craft. On the way to Hong Kong they sailed over the Tubbataha Reef in Philippine waters. To hide their cargo of narcotics they dynamite-fished or cyanide-fished the reef. This harvest process quickly filled the boat's fish wells to conceal the opium by-products. Once safely inside Hong Kong Harbor the illicit bounty could be processed into heroin and sent around the world.

The damage caused to the Tubbataha from this activity needed to be documented. Even though Derek felt he should give some time to Triple C Re in San Francisco he could not pass up a chance to make this trip. On the Tubbataha reef there were over six thousand sea life species! This would be an incredible opportunity.

On a Cook's Bay reef, in the present, Derek drew closer to the venom paralysis tipping point. It was the crossroads of consciousness and unconsciousness. Time was running out. Why did he flash to the South China Sea? Though stunning and remarkable diving, there were no shark epiphanies on this trip. Though it was true that documenting the destruction of the Tubbataha was valuable work, there were no notable aquatic moments to speak of. Derek enjoyed exciting diving with his friend Town, obtained artistic descriptive photos and soaked up a great sun tan. As his life drained away in Cook's Bay why, then, did his mind flash to Manila?

Derek had been a pampered baseball player for much of his life, protected from hard realities. He was twenty-two years old before he knew that home telephones and electricity required a bill to be paid. His professional baseball life was cluttered with attractive girls and private jets. What connection did Derek Dell need to have with reality? He just had to hit the ball far and often. But things in the world weren't as simple as Derek Dell thought.

In many ways the Viet Nam War was no different than other wars. War tends to not only foster damaging drug-smuggling practices, it creates turmoil of all kinds. Long-lasting collateral damage. The drug business often follows the chaos of war. So does extreme poverty. This was the case in South East Asia. A place where life had a far lower value than anything Derek had ever experienced.

Upon their arrival at Manila Airport, Town and Dell were greeted by a man named Richard Deberio. Colonel Deberio would be their host for the time in Manila before setting to sea. Richard was family with Town's new girlfriend.

It had become a tradition for Derek that all dive trips begin with a somewhat luxurious moment in the destination's best spots. Such was the case in Manila. Colonel Deberio saw to it. A caravan of taxis transported Town, Dell, the gear and the colonel to the opulent Hyatt Regency Manila.

Richard was a military man. The Aquino Government in the Philippines was crumbling. Colonel Deberio seemed like the type of soldier that would likely be standing before a firing squad when the politics settled. Town offered the advice that Derek not stand too close to the colonel in case a drive-by shooting was attempted.

Town and Dell checked into rather upscale digs. The walls were paneled in dark wood. Dell could not identify the type. Towels were plush and large. The bed had both feather and foam pillows. The mattress was, of course, deep and comfortable. This would be the perfect place to flop after a big night out. The two met in the hall and headed to the bar to find the colonel.

Derek Dell liked Sapphire gin martinis. It had to be shaken for proper aeration of the liquor and garnished with a lemon peel twist, no olive or onion. He had one on his mind the entire elevator ride down. Richard, Town and Derek sat in a corner booth. The first round was delivered. Richard spoke of the restaurant options. It seemed sushi was on everyone's minds. After a quick exchange with the waiter Richard confirmed he had reservations at the best place in Manila.

The conversation turned to the diving. After they covered the sea life, currents, conditions and the specifics of certain dive sites, Richard began to address safety. Not underwater safety but safety related to piracy and drug smuggling. Dell had dived in the Caribbean where cocaine smugglers frequently passed by dive areas. Frankly, Derek considered those guys a bunch of low-level, under-trained junkies who couldn't rise above the level of boat driver.

The pirates Richard worried about would be experienced military professionals. The ravages of war often left them to use their training as necessary to survive. This was an altogether different risk exposure. Though the other divers aboard the boat would not know it, Richard wanted Town and Derek to know the boat was armed, well armed.

Off the three went. They had a destiny with Saki and Sushi. The colonel had organized a Mercedes limo for the night. Town was relieved it was not a military vehicle. Being in a military vehicle with Colonel Richard Deberio would be like wearing a sign that read, "Please shoot us until you're absolutely certain we're dead."

Their arrival was red carpet. The venue was spectacular. The costumes of the wait staff alone were an artistic and cultural exchange. The cuisine was prepared with detail and care beyond what the three were expecting.

This was not simply food. It was presentation. The sushi chef was the maestro. The ingredients were the musicians. A culinary symphony played out. It took fifteen minutes just to review the types and characteristics of the various sakis the menu offered.

Dish after creative dish arrived at the table. There was no attempt to finish anything. It was now an opportunity to sample many different creations and many different sakis. No matter how you viewed the evening meal, decadence was at dinner that night.

As good fortune would have it, the restaurant bar was one of the best in Manila. It was conveniently located outside the dining area so the live music, karaoke squealing and comedy acts would not disturb anyone's exquisite meal.

Of special note, an extraordinary whorehouse was located just upstairs. The colonel, Derek and Town adjourned to the bar for the heart of the evening. The

Mercedes limo would await their call.

The colonel said, "Derek. I saw you play in a baseball game on TV many years ago."

"Small world," replied Dell. "How'd I do?" Derek asked.

"As I recall, you were ejected from the game," said the colonel.

"Damn," barked Derek. "Of all the ball I played, is that the only part people remember? And is there any place I can go in the world where they don't know about that?" All three laughed. Derek never cared if he was the butt of a joke, as long as everyone laughed. "It is possible that, during moments of enhanced enthusiasm, I may have taken umbrage at one or more of the rules regarding contact in the game of baseball," Dell admitted in his best lawyer voice.

When the last drink was drunk and the last transvestite had sung karaoke, the trio decided to call it a night. Richard said they had one more brief stop to make on the way home. "It is a short walk," said Richard.

Town and Dell moaned about having to catch an early morning flight to the boat. Truth was, they were just nervous about walking outside with the colonel.

They stopped by the limo where Richard accessed the trunk. He produced a plastic bag and a small propane bottle. Down the street they walked.

The neighborhood changed quickly. Tiled roofs and well-kept exteriors faded and tin-roofed shacks took over. The pavement seemed to crumble as they walked. It had not been maintained for years. In fact, nothing in this area seemed to have been maintained. Dell was becoming both confused and a bit alarmed. Town seemed to take things in stride. It felt to Dell like both the colonel and Town knew something he did not.

The three arrived at a house about midway down the tawdry block. A family of five emerged. The colonel presented the bag, which was full of canned goods and some fresh food. The propane was to fire a small camping stove the colonel had provided in an earlier visit.

Introductions were made. Though Town and Dell did not speak Tagalog everyone communicated quite well through smiles, hand gestures and the colonel's slurred interpretations.

Dell was surprised. The colonel was clearly a military man who did the dirty work every government needs done. An assassin, a manipulator and likely corrupted on the turn of a dollar, yet within this creature of such questionable ways was a glimmer of humanity. A pleasant surprise to a wide-eyed Derek Dell. He simply had never seen such things.

The colonel reached into the grocery bag for some tea. He hooked up the propane and boiled some bottled water. Cups were brought out and they all enjoyed some of the colonel's brew. The tea was a welcome taste to Derek.

The youngest daughter of the shabby house looked to be around five years old. Kids seemed to love Derek

Dell and he certainly liked children. Babies would stare at him then break into a smile. Youngsters generally were comfortable approaching him during his baseball days. Derek never really knew why but kids liked him a bunch.

Shyly the daughter emerged from the house, staring at Derek. Dell smiled and gestured her over. The light of the street was dim but Dell could see the kid had lost her left arm. He did not stare and pretended not to be disturbed by the amputation. She quickly warmed up to Dell and, that night, each of them had made a new friend.

Seeing the human side of the colonel was refreshing. It improved Dell's opinion of the man substantially. Now it was absolutely time to go to bed.

The three staggered off. Dell inquired of the colonel, "How did the kid lose her arm? Do you know?"

"Yes," replied Richard. "Her father cut her arm off with a machete in order to make her a more effective beggar."

All progress stopped. Dell literally fell to his knees. He tried to blame his fall on drunkenness but what brought Dell down was pure shock. How could a man do such a thing to his child? thought Dell. How could the living circumstance of any country or any city ever regress to this point? How did the value of life fall to this level? Much like diving with sharks, human suffering was different when you saw it for real.

The baseball player would never be the same. Everything he knew about the world seemed diminished. Living a sheltered life, he had never experienced anything like this. The impact was punishing.

Finally, Dell reached his wood-paneled room. The plush towel, deep soft bed and two types of pillows were all awaiting him. There was even a bit of candy on the bed. He could not stop thinking about the mutilated child and the reason for it. This meant no sleep tonight.

Unimaginable hardship had never crossed Dell's path. Fact is, all he could do was hang his head and cry. He used the two types of pillows to bury his face so the neighbors could not hear his whimpering.

Dell left the Philippines after ten days of successful diving. There were no incidents at sea, no camera failures or bad weather. Dell was, however, certainly changed. He had a new definition of gratitude. He learned the fine points of appreciation and began to see the positive aspects of nearly anything or anybody. In many ways it took a mutilated little girl in Manila to turn a pampered American baseball player into a man. Dell was thirty-five.

Fiji: A New Nation

Of all the remote and exotic destinations Derek Dell had visited, nowhere was as interesting to him as Fiji. The location of Fiji in the South Pacific offered many irresistible diving challenges. The most prolific walls of soft coral found anywhere lived on the reefs of Fiji. This meant current as these fascinating and gorgeous forms of life were filter feeders.

Fiji also lacked the infrastructure to provide proper diver support. Derek had dived Fiji many times. Oily-tasting air or a rusty steel tank could easily frustrate a dive. There was an inherent danger in this type of cavalier attitude toward the mechanics of scuba diving. It generally produces dreadful dive accidents.

Dell did not judge Fiji harshly. He understood that the Republic of Fiji had only existed for a short time. They were feeling their way around internal politics, attempting to produce their first constitution. The British reign over Fiji ended in 1974. Prince Charles presided over the ceremony and an amicable separation was made. Fiji simply needed time to get its house in order.

The most alluring feature of Fiji in Derek Dell's view was its people. Wherever Dell went he made it a point to meet the locals and learn something about them. The British primarily used Fiji as a source of sugar cane. They were not interested in developing Fiji or bringing it forward as a twentieth-century nation. They wanted only sugar. Indigenous Fijians were remarkably self-sufficient. Village life and the ocean provided everything needed to live outside the typical western culture. This kept the old ways alive. Derek Dell loved this aspect of early Fiji. The British, however, needed labor for the cane fields. The answer lay in another former British holding. It was India. The British imported labor from India and solved their cane-field dilemma. The Fijian culture became a blend of two defined segments.

In 1984 Derek received a phone call from Sydney, Australia. It was his friend from many trips to Fiji, Gilroy Kelly. Gilly, as he was known, had a business idea. He wanted to know if Dell was interested in opening a scuba diving business in Fiji. Derek was looking to expand the revenue stream from his dive activities. Selling photos was doing well but he could not afford his lifestyle without Triple C Re. Dell's weakness for sports cars and expensive living was a thirsty beast. He had to increase income. Though Dell cared little about money he generally had the ability to earn it as needed. A diving business would certainly enable Dell to vertically integrate his diving efforts and pull much more money out of the sport. This was a good idea. Gilly and Derek made a date in Fiji.

It took two days for Derek to make his way to Fiji.

The flights went to Hawaii where you changed airlines to head off to Nadi (Nandi) Airport, Fiji. Normally Derek stayed a day or two in Hawaii. He had been traveling there since he was a child. He played in a charity exhibition baseball game there in the early 1970s. Derek had many friends in Hawaii. This trip he went straight through. This was serious business. The excitement was building.

Derek arrived at Nadi early in the morning. He brought little in the way of dive and photo gear as this was primarily a land-based visit. Immigration/Customs was a snap. Fiji offered only one high-end hotel at the time. Dell checked into the Regent of Fiji. The resort was located in Denaru Island. It was an attachment to Viti Levu, the main island. About a thirty-minute cab ride from the airport Derek would be checked in and at the buffet breakfast in no time.

The resort was designed to blend with the lush grounds upon which it sat. The architecture incorporated a Fijian village theme. The well-kept gardens and jungle acreage were spectacular. The island golfing was one of Fiji's featured assets. Though the Regent was certainly a good foot forward, the entire country lacked such fundamentals as television, proper telephone service, broadcast radio and other western niceties. In actual fact, this was part of the charm of the place. In outer Fiji you could live life very similar to how they lived one hundred years ago.

Derek had noticed that wherever he traveled, meetings were always held in a bar. Certainly, there were office meetings with plush conference rooms but on the road, the hotel bar was a staple. Whether the reinsurance business or his diving business, bars were frequent venues. Such was the case for Gilly and Derek in Fiji.

The Fijian people were extremely friendly. Casual contact with a stranger always produced a smile and a, "Bula", a Fijian greeting. It was sincere and had nothing to do with tourism. In fact, tourism was in its infancy in early 1980s Fiji. Fijians were natural ambassadors and a refreshing view of the South Pacific. Dell knew the world of divers would love this place. By the time Dell reached the resort bar he had smiled and said bula fourteen times.

Gilly and another man had arrived and already ordered drinks. It was still early so everyone stuck to juice. Gilly introduced his friend. "This is Jerry Zola," announced Gilly.

"Very pleased to meet you," said Dell with an extended hand.

Jerry replied with a heavy French accent, "Very pleased to meet you too." The three sat down to enjoy a squeeze of the mango and see if they could form a scuba diving company in Fiji!

The conversation was light at first, the kind of chit-chat folks engage in when they meet. Then Jerry said, "Derek, I saw an interview with you on television a few years ago when you were a baseball player. I do not know anything about American baseball but they were questioning you about being ejected from the game. It seems there were many, how you say, "bench-emptying brawls". They sounded upset with you."

Gilly chimed in, "Yeah, Derek. Doesn't the highlight film reel of your career consist of mostly brawls?"

Dell replied in his best lawyer voice, "It might be the case that the essence of my work may have extended the horizon of acceptable behavior in baseball."

Jerry blurted, "Those were exactly the words you used in the interview! I remember."

Gilly said, "Derek is like a toy monkey banging cymbals together. He does it the same every time." It didn't take long. Kidding, chiding and teasing one another became a staple of all future company meetings. This was going to be fun!

Jerry and Gilly were both Qantas airline crew. They were highly trained in the travel and hospitality business and would be invaluable to any tourist dive business. Jerry was also a PADI Master Instructor. PADI stands for Professional Association of Dive Instructors and pretty much sets the rules for scuba diving. His level of technical training was not found at any dive operation in the early days of Fiji. Gilly, apart from his professional contribution, was literally the funniest person Derek Dell had ever known. His quick wit, clever quips and straight up jokes were a massive contribution to the forming company. Everyone who met Gilly liked him. Adding Derek's camera work to the talent pool made the new company already more skilled than any other in Fiji and it wasn't even formed yet.

They had agreed to partner and form the company. Now the question was, where shall it base? Fiji is composed of over three-hundred islands. The diving differs in each area. The guys decided that locating the operation on Mana Island in the Mamanucca (Mamanutha) area would be ideal. Mana had good access (about an hour's ferry ride from Nadi), some of Fiji's best weather and a steady supply of guests who could take scuba lessons or day boat dive trips. The other key feature was the ability for the three founders to market the products in the US and Australia. The advantage to the resort on Mana was, indeed, that overseas marketing ability. This would be a mutually beneficial relationship between the resort and the dive concession. The three decided that it was now late enough to set aside the mango juice and have a celebratory drink. Only one task remained. What would they call the new company?

The boys pondered one name after another as they downed one drink after another. Derek Dell was not a big drinker. The two Aussie guys could put Dell under the table without slurring a word. For his own protection Dell thought a name had better come up soon or he might not be sober enough to cast a vote. Derek blurted out, "Aqua Trek. Yes, Aqua Trek, Ocean Sports Adventures."

Gilly and Jerry became silent, staring into the

table. Dell could feel the wheels in their heads churning over the name. The two Aussies raised their heads with smiles and said, "Yes, we have a name!"

Gilly's connections on Mana Island were quite high up. The resort was owned by a Japanese company and Gilly's Qantas training had schooled him in the protocols of business with the Japanese. The meeting was set for the three Aqua Trek directors to visit Mana.

The boys caught the morning ferry for Mana Island. The meeting itself was uneventful. In keeping with the Japanese style of business the terms of the arrangement were pretty much agreed to prior to the visit. Gilly had done his preliminary work very effectively. This meant the meeting was mostly ceremonial.

There was an existing dive operator on Mana Island. A small neglected concession, it had one rather amazing employee. That was dive master Apisai Bati.

The Legend of Apisai Bati

Apisai (Api) Bati was an indigenous Fijian from the island of Tavua in Western Fiji. It is located a short distance from Mana. Api's village lived life in the traditional Fijian style, devoid of western culture and its complications. Api's first pair of shoes didn't arrive until he was sixteen years old. Likely the only reason he got a pair was to attend church and pursue his ministry. Api was a man of God and a disciple of Jesus Christ. An enormous man, Api was a gifted athlete. His strength and speed made him a natural for Fiji's popular rugby team.

Api, however, was not interested in sports. His devotion to faith, family and diving were everything he needed to be joyous about life. He was exactly that. It showed in his smile, gentle demeanor and personal confidence.

Gilly, Jerry and Derek left the meeting with the management of Mana Island Resort and immediately sought out Api. All the guys had dived with Api in the past so they unanimously invited him to join the Aqua Trek team. Loved and respected by anyone who met him, Api was an example of Fiji at its finest. The boys of Aqua Trek viewed Api as the heart of the business.

Apisai Bati worked on Mana Island with Aqua Trek until the day he died. The growth of the company and Api's incredible feats underwater resulted in his gaining international fame and acknowledgment as an original shark wrangler and adventure diver. At the core of his gift in animal handling was his powerful faith and devotion to God. The fact is, people like Derek Dell were humbled in Api's presence.

Over the years Derek would ask much of Api. The two planned and executed numerous dive strategies, animal handling demonstrations and photographic events. Api's robust energy for each project resulted in the development of an international reputation of excellence for Aqua Trek and celebrity status for Api. Api became the subject of books, television specials and industry promotions. His giant feet were imprinted on T-shirts and sold worldwide. He could carry six tanks when loading the boat. Derek knew no-one in the world who could do that. Despite fame and recognition, Api never changed or became anything other than a simple, gentle man of God. Of note, Api never commented to Derek about his abysmal career in baseball.

Derek Dell, during his career, had dived everywhere from the North Pole to the South Pacific. Worked with elite professionals of all kinds and in every imaginable place. No-one Dell ever met was as special as Apisai Bati. Api was a tribute to humanity.

A Fijian funeral boat holds the casket and only a few select family. It visits the nearby islands permitting all to say farewell. Derek Dell was honored to be invited on Api's funeral boat.

September 13, 1986

Today, on a Cook's Bay reef Derek Dell struggles to hang on to consciousness. His mind has flashed through many events, many people and covered many years. September 13, 1986, brings a smile to even the face of a drowning Derek Dell. This is the birthday of his daughter Lydia.

Things were going pretty good for Derek. Triple C Re was growing and Aqua Trek was expanding to additional locations. He opened a booking office for Aqua Trek in San Francisco, right next door to Triple C Re. Derek and then wife Ann were living in a huge house in Moss Beach. The perfect time to have a baby. Of course, the birth of a child changes everything for young parents. They scramble to adjust and ultimately become comfortable with the necessities for a new child and their important role as parents.

Word gets out to Fiji. "Bosso Levu," as Derek became known, was a father. Everyone at Aqua Trek shared the joy of Lydia's arrival. They even named their primary dive boat the *Lidilailai* (Little Lydia) in homage.

The next year continued to be kind to Derek. The trajectory of his career was demanding but rewarding. He concentrated his diving on just California and Fiji.

Lydia was traveling with him overseas when only three months old. Derek and Ann never hesitated to surrender Lydia to the loving arms of Fijian ladies. Everyone in Fiji loved Lidilailai. She would grow up knowing Fiji in its original glory in the days before TV, the internet or McDonald's arrived to shrink the world. Derek believed this was a rare gift to give to his daughter.

Opportunity Knocks

In late 1986 two American Titans turned their eyes on Fiji. One of them was *Skin Diver* magazine. It was part of print media giant Peterson Publishing and literally owned the dive magazine market. The other was Continental Airline and their wholesale division, Continental Pacific Vacations. Together they were planning a scuba diving marketing campaign focused on the new paradise destination of Fiji.

This was an incredible opportunity for Aqua Trek. They could access the huge American market of scuba divers: over eleven million potential clients. The boys of Aqua Trek were enthused but tempered their excitement because there was a complication, a hitch, if you will.

Mana Island was located in Western Fiji. That is where the best beaches, finest weather and most resorts were located. It is not, however, where Fiji's legendary soft corals are found. In the north of Fiji was the Rainbow Reef and in Central Fiji, Beqa (Benga) Lagoon. These were the fabled soft coral dives of Fiji. How would Aqua Trek get its market share? Mana Island, with its warm, calm western waters, was a teaching boom for Aqua Trek. They processed thousands of students each year. The visiting

Americans, however, would be advanced dive travelers, satisfied with only the best diving. The investment each Fiji dive operators had to make was substantial. So was the importance of market share.

The Aqua Trek guys were worried. Dell had an idea. The solution rested in two strategic moves. First, the boys would scout dive the outer Malololailai Barrier Reef. Outside the reef was a twelve-thousand-foot drop-off. Currents from the deep blue brought cold water nutrients to the surface. This was the reef that surrounded Mana Island and the other members of the Mamanucca chain. Its complexity and distance meant it was never dived by the resort scuba operators. Most of their holiday divers were looking for easy splash-downs. This area was for the serious and skilled.

Adding to the challenges of the deep barrier reef was the long-held practice of resorts dumping their garbage off the outer drop. This despicable practice not only offended environmental senses it drew the muscular and dangerous bull sharks to the area. This would be a hard reef to master but could provide the Americans with the dramatic diving they expected from the virgin South Pacific.

The second product that Dell proposed was the development of a shark dive in the waters near Mana Island. He planned to create an experience like nothing else offered in Fiji. Advanced American divers would pay well for the opportunity to safely encounter numerous sharks on a close but controlled basis.

The course was clear. These special dive adventures were the means by which the company would get market share from the American promotional endeavor. This would put the company in the eye of international divers and launch Aqua Trek on its way!

Nothing Aqua Trek ever did in the waters near Mana Island occurred without Apisai Bati leading the way. He was the master. Everyone else was a follower. Api and the three directors headed to the Castaway Wall to scout dive the first product. The Castaway Wall was the best access point to the outer Malololailai Barrier Reef. It was also where Castaway Island dumped its garbage.

The four plunged off the *Lidilailai*, anchored in the shallows and headed to the drop off. Derek rarely entered the water without a camera. This dive, he carried two.

They were all pleased to see that no signs of dumped garbage existed. The resorts made sure they dumped well off the reef in the deep blue. Their trash would settle thousands of feet below.

As the divers descended the outer wall there were no signs of soft corals. Soft corals required currents to feed. The pounding of the ocean's force on a barrier reef like Malololailai proved too much for the development of the delicate corals. Dell did, however, discover several fan corals in the area. They were a heartier filter feeder and could survive the tidal turbulence of the outer reef. His cameras lit up.

If Api had any weakness as a diver it was that his giant size caused him to use a tank of air quickly. Dell had a lesser version of the same problem. Api and Jerry were near empty and slowly ascending. Gilly was also low and headed up stopping at a fan coral along the way. Derek snapped a photo of Gilly inspecting the fan. This photo turned out to be one of Derek Dell's career favorites. It was highly published.

Dell's relaxed dive style allowed him to shoot several photos while using little air. He found himself in the water alone. He moved down the outer reef at a depth of ninety-five feet.

Derek could usually tell his depth by the mere sound of air leaving his regulator. Different depth and pressures produce different sounds. Over time Dell never needed to consult a depth gauge as the regulator's expulsion told him all he needed to know. This allowed him to attend more to photo composition and camera settings.

Slowly swimming along the reef, he came upon a large crack. It appeared to be around twenty feet wide and fifty feet from top to bottom. The crack seemed to go deeply through the reef, into the inner lagoon where the *Lidilailai* was anchored. It begged for Dell to swim through.

The entrance was bracketed by fan corals of large stature. This was a good sign. As he moved into the crevice, he found the soft corals the boys so anxiously desired. Protection offered by the gaping hole allowed the soft corals to flourish. The outer reef deep water currents flowing through the crack would feed this garden lavishly. Dell shot the area thoroughly.

At this point Derek was entirely lost. He knew if he simply reversed course and swam out of the crevice the same way he came in, he would soon break into the outer reef and open ocean. From there he could surface and find the anchored dive boat and his fellow divers.

As he swam toward the outer reef the building inward current began to challenge his kick. Dell was noted for his legs and the dive-kick they produced. Strong legs were a by-product of being a big-league catcher. He could easily overcome the current but he would use a lot of air doing so.

He moved forward only to see a bull shark entered the crack from Dell's planned exit point. The two would meet head to head about one hundred feet from the outer reef exit point.

The animal was large, ten feet or more. It was undulating from side to side in a somewhat exaggerated fashion. Normally this was pre-attack behavior but Derek optimistically chalked it up to necessary effort for the shark to handle the current. Dell was the focus of the shark's attention and eye contact was solid.

The bull moved toward Dell in an investigatory style. Derek backed into the reef, packing himself as deeply as he could. His camera was on fire. The flashing strobe seemed to annoy the apex predator and it eventually moved past Derek.

Dell knew there was no real risk. Once solid eye contact is made with a big breed shark their genetic programming tells them the element of surprise is lost. Large sharks burn mega energy moving their thousand-pound bodies around. The efficiency of their genetic perfection prefers the element of surprise to feed with little effort. Chasing and fighting for food is a last resort for these monsters.

With all that duly noted, Derek did not overlook the fact that he was alone, ninety feet underwater in an enclosed space with a curious bull shark. It was a friendly pass. The shark and diver went their separate ways in peace.

Adventure and the unknown is what exploratory diving is all about. As time passed the Aqua Trek staff would continue to explore the Malololailai Barrier Reef until it became a safe and exciting destination for any level of diver. The practice of dumping garbage was discontinued and the area resorts all cooperated in the formation of one of Fiji's first marine park. This was Aqua Trek leadership at its finest. Derek was proud to be its managing director.

The Sharks of Supermarket Reef

The second product needed to compete in the American marketing campaign was the show-stopper. At that time there were few places on earth where a diver could safely encounter sharks close up and in a controlled event. Derek Dell believed the tactics he learned in French Polynesia while diving with Christophe could be imported to Fiji.

That afternoon Derek, Gilly and Api met in the Aqua Trek Dive Bure (booraay). Jerry had left for Australia to go on duty with Qantas. The planning commenced. Dell knew that an essential for a shark dive is that the area selected is a robust ecosystem. This will ensure the sharks are in the general area.

The Supermarket dive site already used by Aqua Trek came to mind immediately. Relatively shallow, the Supermarket got its name because of the variety of fish inhabiting the reef. There were also light currents creating a drift into which blood from a speared fish could be inserted.   Api would work the speargun, Dell the camera and Gilly would act as safety observer. Sharks love sneaking up on their prey. Another set of eyes was essential.

All agreed that banging metal on their tanks would be a danger signal. Heads up three-sixty. Sound underwater travels in all directions. You could not tell from where the danger alert was coming. That's why you had to look three hundred, sixty degrees. Make that important eye contact if a shark approached too closely. One item remained.

Api needed a new speargun. His old gear was worn. It had provided many meals for the Bati family over the years, but all dive gear expires. Salt water is hard on everything. The boys adjourned to a Nadi town store.

Api grabbed the most impressive rig Dell had ever seen. The bait fish Api would be seeking didn't stand a chance. The accuracy of a new gun would permit Api to quickly obtain and control his target. The control part was important in that the vibration of the speared fish was an attraction signal, just like blood.

The spear was launched by three lengths of surgical tubing. The tension was so taut it took a man of Api's unusual strength just to cock the weapon. Derek was embarrassed to even try. Gilly disappeared to another aisle, pretending to examine flip-flops. They would let Api handle the gun. The boys would meet at the dive bure early the next morning.

The morning was stunning. Most of the island was still sleeping. Derek and Gilly walked down the crescent beach of white sand headed to the dive bure. Their pace was relaxed and they said little. Each diver had gear slung over their shoulder. Cameras, regulators and the like were dangling across Dell's chest. The water was dead flat in the lagoon. The conditions were perfect.

As they approached the dive bure the guys could hear music. As a devout Christian, Api often played his favorite gospel tapes after hours. This morning was a capella four-part harmony. Both Derek and Gilly enjoyed the sound as they approached the bure. "Everything's gonna be all right, when Jesus comes", sang the group. "Everyone's gonna shout their troubles over. When Jesus comes", went the verse.

Api eyed the boys walking up the beach and silenced the music. Derek said, "Hey, Api, turn that back up. Gilly and I love the Persuasions. One of my favorite groups." The music had a relaxing effect on all three divers. With the music's volume at a conversational level, the guys began the dive plan review.

"You nervous?" Gilly asked.

"Let me see," responded Dell. "We're headed to a notoriously active dive site, spearing a fish with that cannon Api's toting, stimulating the feeding impulse in sharks that pack-hunt and we really don't know a damn thing about what we're doing. Yes, I'm nervous." Dell further declared, "Far as I'm concerned, if Api wants to Jesus up a little this morning, that's fine with me. We should probably do the same," Dell suggested. The three loaded the *Lidilailai* and headed out.

Gilly moored the boat carefully. It would be empty during the dive and he certainly didn't want it drifting away. Their entry was relaxed and descent direct. All three had dived this area several times. They hovered near the reef wall at about fifty feet deep. Dell readied the camera, Gilly positioned himself and Api moved off the wall, seeking bait.

The Supermarket delivered. From the abyss emerged a large school of barracuda. The eyes of all three met and smiles came over their faces. The barracuda were exactly what the divers needed. Api drew back the surgical tubing and cocked the gun with all three lines. The shot would be explosive.

He swam directly into the school and fired. The school was so thick he didn't need to aim very carefully. In fact, it would have been hard to miss. Gilly and Derek could feel the vibration as the spear displaced water, racing toward the fish.

The strike was concussive. A large barracuda literally exploded in the water. Dell could not identify a piece of the animal larger than a nickel. All that remained of the barracuda was a red mist drifting down the reef. Again, all three divers made eye contact.

These guys were all from different cultures, different hemispheres and different ways. They had one personality trait in common. Each had a highly developed sense of humor. They could find comedy in nearly any situation. The first to succumb was Derek. He began to laugh at the preposterousness of Api's overkill with the speargun. After one glance at that, both Api and Gilly lost it and burst into underwater laughter.

With that, the divers had to surface. The

contortions of their faces during out-loud laughter broke the dive mask seal from their cheeks. Sea water flooded in. All three arrived at the surface gasping for air, with their heads thrown back in hilarity. "Perhaps a little too much gun, eh, Api?" laughed Dell. The divers continued joking as once Gilly got started it was hard to stop him. Gilly was in rare form. His comedic observations of the dive events thus far had the other two in stitches. Derek and Api were an easy audience to begin with.

The moment was interrupted when Derek noticed the trio were surrounded by circling sharks, responding to the kill. Dorsal fins were breaking the surface and the boys had better compose themselves and get underwater quickly. When confronted with circling sharks you want to be underwater so eye contact and clear observations can be made.

Though the fate of the barracuda was humorous, the outcome was effective. The sharks were responsive to the red mist. It was enough to draw their curiosity but not to drive a frenzy. These were bronze whaler reef sharks, white-tips and the occasional tiger shark. The concern was for the white-tips. White-tips hunt in packs. They work together creating mad, rapid chaos in the reef fish they hunt. The prey flees the mouth of one shark and is driven into the mouth of another. The chomping sound is frightening, a reminder of the power that resides in the jaws of each shark. The event rises near the level of frenzy. Faster darting made it impossible to keep an eye on all the animals. If a full frenzy were to break out the sharks will begin hitting anything and everything in their path. This had to be avoided at all cost.

The red mist had vanished from the area. The sharks began to settle down and an increase in comfort came over the divers. The boys decided not to press their luck and called it a day. On the *Lidilailai* heading back to the dive bure they agreed to keep their efforts secret for a while. There was no telling how the area resorts would react if word got out Aqua Trek was wrangling sharks on Supermarket Reef.

That was how it began. From that day forward the Aqua Trek team perfected the shark dive. Api's skill and reputation earned worldwide acclaim. The Americans were just the beginning.

In the succeeding years divers from every corner of the planet visited Mana Island, Fiji to dive the Supermarket Shark Dive. Sheiks, kings, movie stars and regular divers all sought the Aqua Trek product.

To handle the politics with the other resorts, Aqua Trek allowed any resort dive boat to join the dive. Spreading the wealth to competitors was a good idea. All the teams worked as professionals to ensure the safety of the event. This was symbiosis at its highest level. From the sharks beneath to the Aqua Trek guys above, all worked together to strike a sustainable balance between these prehistoric creatures and the modern world of the mid-1980s.

War Gets in the Way

The beginning of 1987 was looking good for Aqua Trek. Derek was bouncing back and forth between San Francisco and Fiji on a regular basis. Lydia was along as often as possible. Triple C Re was doing well too. The side-by-side offices of Aqua Trek and Triple C Re offered convenience and efficiency for Derek's San Francisco presence.

Dell was starting to feel certain stresses he did not know how to handle. Most of his life he basked in the benefits of doing something special. Baseball, racing cars and now shark-wrangling had always made him feel good about his spectrum of life. He took comfort in the fact that he engaged life at an aggressive level. That was important to Derek Dell. On the other hand, Lydia's birth opened Derek's mind to the glory of normal life. Parenting Lydia was Derek Dell's greatest joy. The yin and yang of that lifestyle was something he had to deal with.

Maintaining the balance often challenged Dell in ways he didn't handle well. Was he an adventurer? Living a dynamic existence only few can imagine? Or should he focus on being a good husband, reinsurance guy and, above all, father? Embrace the normal life in its entirety? Leave aside the foolish high-risk diving?

The conclusion was that his soul required both. He was not always driven by cold logic. If you did not answer your passions you could die with too many regrets. It was as simple as that for Derek Dell.

He spent more time away from Ann and the monster house they built in Moss Beach. His dog Franco was his constant companion and a champion of devotion. The two hung out at the beach. Dell surfed and Franco paraded up and down, sniffing everything while keeping Dell in sight. Something was wrong. Derek Dell did not feel right.

In the May of '87 Derek Dell was at his office in San Francisco. A call was coming in from Fiji. That was a rough task in 1987. It was Jerry Zola. He was on Mana Island and reporting there was a coup at the Government House in Suva. The Government of the Republic of Fiji was changing hands by military force! Dell was stunned. News feeds out of Fiji were nearly unheard-of at that time. Derek anguished over the state of his business and the future of Fiji. All the work they had done, the risks they took and the joy they shared could dissolve in the confusion of war.

The coup hit the dive industry hard. The American State Department put Fiji on the "do not travel" list. The momentum of the *Skin Diver* magazine promotion was evaporating in the sun. Though the boats were near empty, the Aqua Trek boys continued working with the sharks. Down time was used to repair gear, paint and clean the entire operation up to five-star fashion.

In California Derek had another problem to face. Ann wanted a divorce. Derek was not surprised as they had grown in different directions. Both of them wanted only the happiness of an infant Lydia. Things were amicable. Amicable or not, it looked like the war in Fiji and the war in the Dell household were getting in the way of happiness in both hemispheres.

Dell went to Fiji. It was important for him to show leadership during the difficulties of the coup. The Aqua Trek guys were quick to rally behind Dell when the news of his divorce got out. A scenario of mutual nurturing developed. Fiji nursed Derek, and he nursed Fiji.

The dive industry in Fiji needed a way to survive. It was agreed amongst the various dive operators that a meeting would be held at the Pacific Harbor Resort in Beqa. This was the launch point for world renowned Beqa Lagoon soft coral diving. The grounds were lush, the bars were open and the meeting well attended.

The sales guys from both *Skin Diver* magazine and Continental Airlines were in the bar with their corporate expense accounts set on unlimited. By the time Derek checked into his room it was after six. He cleaned up and headed to the bar to share in that corporate love flowing off the salesmen.

Derek entered the bar, greeted his colleagues and ordered his favorite beer, Fiji Gold. He sat at the bar next to a stunning blonde woman from Australia. Derek was unsure if he was ready to date or, for that matter, even had the courage to speak to a woman. He was actually quite insecure when it came to girls.

Dell felt an uncomfortable burn down the right side of his body. It ran from head to toe. He turned to find its source. It was the stare of the blonde next door. She was sufficiently wasted by six-thirty p.m. to lust after Dell in an uninhibited drunk-girl style Derek had not seen since the Sumer of Love in San Francisco. Upon notice, Derek discovered this girl was just plain gorgeous. Even fall-down drunk, with her hair having dangled in a puddle of her own vomit, she was hot!

Mercifully, Derek was rescued from himself by an indigenous Fijian who presented his hand to shake.

"My name is Emanueli Baralavela," said the Fijian. "People call me Vela," he added.

Secrets

"Very nice to meet you, Vela," said Dell. "I'm Derek Dell," he added.

"I know who you are, Mr. Dell. Everyone in Fiji knows you," Vela smiled.

"Okay, Vela, first things first," said Dell. "Please don't call me Mr. Dell. Derek will do nicely." Vela happily complied. The two instantly liked one another. Vela said he had a business proposition for Derek and wondered if Dell had dinner plans. Other than the blonde Aussie, Derek had no plans at all. The two new friends walked to the main dining room and organized a table in the outdoor section. The restaurant was rather elegant but the informal style of dress in the Fiji Islands added casual comfort to the evening.

Vela said, "Derek, I saw a video of you playing baseball on one occasion. I do not know anything about American baseball. Is all that fighting and bench-emptying part of the game?" he asked in all innocence. "I was told you were ejected.".

Dell started in with his normal lawyerly response to comments on the details of his baseball career, then stopped and said, "Wait a minute. I don't have any legal exposure over my baseball career here in Fiji. Let's just say I played the game a little outside the rules," Derek lamented. Derek was confused as to why Vela had taken the time and effort to study Derek's failed baseball career of years ago.

Vela explained the some of the young men in his church were discussing Derek, the American who brought shark diving to Fiji. "They said you were the best diver they have seen," Vela commented.

Dell replied, "Are you kidding? No-one dives like the Fijian guys at Aqua Trek. Besides, they've never even seen my A game," Dell joked. Humor was part of Derek Dell's persona. It put people at ease when they seemed nervous around Derek.

Vela began discussing Derek's dive skills. Though he was interested in the sharks, they had nothing to do with his business proposition. Derek was surprised at the detail of Vela's knowledge and information about him. Even matters relative to Dell's life in America were known to Vela. Dell was now more than curious. A Fijian guy wanders up to him, knows more about his life than is explainable and says he has a business proposition. Actually, Dell was getting nervous.

Dinner progressed and the conversation meandered. Finally, Vela seemed ready to get down to business. Vela was from the village of Maleqa (Malenga) located up the Nausori River in the highlands of Fiji. The highlands are quite a different place than the beach areas of Fiji. Up there, life is lived by reliance on the land. Beach area villages rely on the sea.

Dell was interested in how Vela found his way to the diving business, coming from the highlands. Vela explained that, like many Fijians, he had family in New Zealand. He had dual citizenship and had been in the New Zealand Military. Vela was a member of the New Zealand Special Air Services (NZSAS). Dell ceased eating and met Vela's eyes in concentrated listening. SAS are equivalent Navy SEALS in America. Vela's training in the SAS would have been some of the finest in the world.

"With your kind of training and dual citizenship, why are you back in Fiji living village life in the highlands?" Dell asked. Vela responded that he preferred his life in Fiji. His church, family and island roots were very important. However, like all people everywhere, he had to make a living. With the coup and general lack of economic opportunity in Fiji, Vela used his training and connections to do work away from Fiji. The pay was sufficient to provide a very nice lifestyle for his family in Fiji.

Vela put down his utensils, adjusted his chair to face Derek more directly and asked if Derek was political. Dell replied that he had never even voted and thought politicians were simply chronic liars addicted to power. Vela didn't seem surprised. In fact, Vela looked like he already knew that Dell cared little about governments.

Vela explained that the American/Russian Cold War which had been ongoing for decades was very technology-based. The Americans were tracking

Russian submarines with hydrophones (underwater microphones). The old Russian diesel subs made quite a clatter as they cut through the water. The hydrophones were able to detect their sounds and track the direction they were heading. Vela explained that this network of hydrophones was called SOSUS (Sound Surveillance System). There were similar systems placed in the South Pacific by Australia and New Zealand governments as allies of the Americans.

These systems were essentially obsolete. Most of the Russian submarines were now nuclear and tracking activity was done with satellites. The hydrophone network was being used by marine biologists, on a limited basis, to track whales. Their purpose was to identify the direction of pods, locate breeding and feeding areas and establish data base information.

Dell's interest was piqued. "I had no idea things like that were out there," Dell confessed. "Where do I fit in?" he inquired. Vela explained that these systems needed maintenance and the navy did not feel they could do the work. Navy presence would signal the location of the devices. Despite the obsolete nature of the hydrophones they were still secret government property in secret government locations. The Pacific Ocean covers nearly a third of the entire planet. Island nations are only tiny specks of land found here and there in the vastness of the Pacific. Vela was correct. Any navy activity would stick out like a whore in church.

As the evening progressed so did the intensity of the discussions. Dell was entirely captivated. Vela was equally captivated as he saw Derek's interest grow. Technical issues came up. Dell asked how deep the hydrophones were located. Vela looked away. That particular subject added to the complexity of the dive. The devices were located at different depths but most were in the two hundred to two hundred fifty-foot zone. Dell looked challenged but not defeated when those numbers came up. The amount of time a scuba diver can remain at such depths is so limited, Dell wondered how any sort of work could be done. This was deep and dangerous. Perfect conditions for getting the bends. Vela had an answer for that but it required a story.

The Ivy Bells Divers

Vela told of a secret joint American CIA/NSA/Navy project that was implemented in the 1970s. It was called the Ivy Bells Mission. A specially-equipped submarine, the *U.S.S. Halibut*, was sent to Russian territorial waters in the Sea of Okhotsk. Any foreign vessel was strictly off limits in those waters as the Russian Pacific Fleet Headquarters was accessible from there. The American sub entered the area seeking the location of Russian underwater communication cables.

The American Navy and General Electric Corp had developed a device that could be attached to underwater telephone cables, allowing conversations to be intercepted. The Russians had their own hydrophone systems and were vigilant in listening for intruders into the Sea of Okhotsk. The *Halibut* moved in anyhow.

The boat eventually located the cables. They rested in about four hundred feet of water. Divers exited the boat and installed the General Electric Corp device. Dell questioned the sanity of diving on scuba at those remarkable depths. Nitrogen narcosis would set in quickly. Some called this rapture of the deep. How did the divers survive? How were their mental faculties functioning sufficiently to install a complex piece of spy gear? Dell was enthralled.

The restaurant was closed. Vela and Derek had not noticed. Fijians would not interrupt a conversation over a simple matter of closing time. They patiently awaited notice by Derek and Vela. The two made their apologies to the staff. Time just got away from them. The conversation moved to a sitting area in the hotel lobby. Coffee was served.

Details Emerge

Vela asked if Derek had ever heard the term, "nitrox". Dell had not.

Vela discussed how the composition of the air we were breathing was about 80/20. Ambient air is 80% nitrogen and 20% oxygen. Simple to understand. Every diver knew that. Nitrox merely changed the percentages and increased the amount of oxygen. The more oxygen in the mix the less your chance of getting narcosis or the bends. The Ivy Bells divers used nitrox. They were the first. "That is how we will complete the work we need to do," Vela said. "We will use nitrox to enable our bodies to tolerate such depths and maintain the hydrophones."

Dell asked, "What percentage of oxygen will we be using?"

Vela replied, "Probably 36%."

"Wow," said Dell. "At 36% I'm not gonna even need my A game!"

Vela smiled. From what he had heard, Vela thought Derek might be right.

Dell said there were three important questions that needed answering. Why were they interested in him and how much would he be paid? Of most importance, who would he be working for?

Vela explained that, due to the sensitive nature of work, Dell had been vetted. This explained Vela's knowledge of Derek's baseball history and the details of Dell's life in America. Derek felt a bit uncomfortable at the notion of being secretly examined so closely without his knowledge. And, by the way, who was doing the examining?

Apart from the obvious skills in technical diving, Vela spoke of Dell's outside-the-lines way of doing things. That style might work well in this type of job. At those depths and conditions improvisation may come in handy. Of more importance though, the work must be kept secret and the locations remain unknown. Dell's career as an underwater photographer and South Pacific dive operator entitled him to go anywhere in South Pacific waters, never raising the slightest question. Stealth activity would be a cinch for Derek.

Vela then addressed the subject of compensation. Though the coup in Fiji hurt Aqua Trek's business, Vela worried that Derek might not need money as Triple C Re was doing well. Derek's response was surprising to Vela as the vetting that was done apparently did not reveal everything.

Dell was clear.

"Are you kidding? Dell exclaimed. "I've got the IRS up my ass and my ex-wife's lawyer going in down my throat. They're meeting in my stomach and giving me indigestion."

In all innocence, Vela asked, "Is the IRS some sort

of disease of the anus?"

Dell looked up and smiled. "In my case, yes." Dell told Vela the IRS was the equivalent of the Inland Revenue Department in Fiji. "They are the tax man," Dell informed him. Vela now understood Dell's comment and dilemma.

"We are paid USD $5,000 per dive plus any expenses you incur."

Dell winced. That seemed like a lot of money for a twenty-minute dive. There must be more to it than he thought.

Derek thirsted for more information. Who would Dell be working for? Vela spoke of a group of military-trained South Pacific islanders like himself. They hired out to various governments to perform necessary services. They lived all over the South Pacific. Dell immediately pegged them as mercenaries. Vela agreed that, technically, they were mercenaries but mostly they were villager who preferred family life, church and island living. Derek still had the vision of men who considered chloroform and Stockholm Syndrome foundations of a good marriage. Their only religion would be the Church of Smith and Wesson. Vela was eager to convince Derek otherwise.

He invited Derek to visit his village to meet Ratu Vunni Baleqaqa (Balenganga). Ratu means chief or leader in Fijian. Ratu Vunni was not only Vela's boss, he was the Ratu of the village where Vela and his family lived.

Respect and tradition were important modes of conduct in authentic Fijian village life. This was particularly important since Dell was kavelaqi (Kavelangi — Caucasian). On the way to his room Derek stopped by reception. He requested someone obtain yaqona root. This is the root of the pepper plant used to make kava, a ceremonial drink containing a mild narcotic. Kava is used by indigenous people all over the South Pacific. In Fiji kava is used in leadership, business or guest ceremonies, called Sevu Sevu.

In the village the main bure is the equivalent of the town hall in America. Fijians call this bure kalau. It's the location of the Sevu Sevu ceremony that opens a meeting. The guest will offer kava root as a gesture of honor for being invited to the village. While the leaders of the village sit circled on the floor with the guest, younger men act as servers and go to work. The root kava brought by the guest is unprocessed. This shows the greatest level of respect and understanding of Fijian tradition. Processed powder would never do for Derek Dell. Grinding and drying the unprocessed root takes a good deal of time. The young servers will take the root away, bring already processed powder and begin the ceremony.

A large bowl called a tanoa is fetched by the servers. In the tanoa are coconut shells cut in half to act as a cups or "bilo". The servers place the kava in a cheesecloth rag to make a large teabag. Warm water is added to the tanoa and the cheesecloth milked of the kava's nectar.

The first bilo is offered to the guest. A server fills the cup and kneels in front of the guest. The server extends his arms with the bilo while lowering his eyes to the guest. Posturing of this type shows respect to the visitor. Receiving the bilo is structured as well. The guest must clap their hands twice. Now, we're not talking some wimpy golf-course clap, it must be palm to palm and muscular. After downing the bilo the guest claps three times more. The Ratu is next. The process repeats itself until the entire circle has been served.

After the initial round the servers will leave. They remain on call. The men in the circle will continue to drink kava but will help themselves. You must empty the contents of the bilo so it is best to declare either "high tide" or "low tide" when filling the bilo. Derek Dell never met a drug he didn't like. It was always high tide in Derek's bilo.

The next morning Vela and Derek met for breakfast. When Vela saw the yaqona root he smiled. Vela knew Derek understood and appreciated the culture of Fiji.

The Village of Maleqa

The Nasouri River joins the ocean in the town of Suva. It's a short cab ride from the hotel. A young man from Maleqa was waiting for Vela and Derek in a Yamaha Long Boat. These were the most practical and versatile craft in Fiji. The ride upriver was slow enough that Derek could enjoy the sights. Like most rivers in developing nations the Nasouri was used by villagers for a number of purposes. Transportation, laundry, and fishing were the primary purposes of the trip.

As the boat progressed upstream the population density thinned out considerably. No longer could buildings be seen. The land was rich and lush. Villages were located away from the river in the highland jungles. Tributary streams to the Nasouri served drinking water needs.

The Yamaha arrived at a nearly invisible boat dock. From there they walked a twenty-minute journey up to the village. Derek and Vela were greeted and immediately directed to the bure kalau. As they walked through the village Derek could feel the eyes of its inhabitants fixed on him. At that time in Fiji there were few kavelaqi visiting highland villages.

Derek and Vela entered the bure kalau and took

their seats on the woven mats covering the floor. Soon Ratu Vunni would appear and the Sevu Sevu began. Normally Ratu Vunni would be accompanied by village elders who collectively represent the people. Today Ratu Vunni had younger men at his side: obvious members of his team. The day's conversation would not be about the village. At the conclusion of the ceremonial kava proceedings the servers became sentries and stood on either side of the bure entrance.

Ratu Vunni opened the conversation expressing his gratitude for Derek making the trip up the Nasouri. Derek courteously nodded in reply. Vunni then explained that he represented a team of workers who did various jobs using their military training. The story paralleled the talk Derek had with Vela the night before. Vunni's job was to broker the work to the proper people on his team. There were other managers like him around the South Pacific. Some jobs required more than one team due to the enormity of the Pacific. Vunni's own experience was impressive. Not only had Vunni been SAS, he was a commander! Derek could tell from Vunni's manner of speech, posture and presence that this man was well trained and well educated. Dell could not understand why Vunni and Vela embraced a near-primitive lifestyle. Most Fijians Derek knew were eager to seek western ways. It was refreshing to see tradition and heritage continued.

Derek wanted to know why they were interested in him. He had no military training or skills, nor did he live in the South Pacific full time. Moreover, Derek was not interested in performing any military-style functions at all. He certainly made it clear several times that he would not hurt anyone and absolutely would not kill anyone. Derek claimed he was merely a broken-down baseball player and joked, "Does your village need a catcher?"

Vunni explained that the jobs they had for Derek had little to do with conflict. He and Vela would do nothing more than service hydrophones to ensure they were functioning properly. Though obsolete as surveillance tools, the hydrophones' locations and very existence was still secret.

Dell was approached because he offered a unique ability. Derek Dell could go anywhere in the South Pacific as an underwater photographer. This freedom of movement had value. Derek was a known cameraman and dive operator which allowed him to be virtually invisible as he traveled throughout the South Pacific. Heading out to sea from any harbor in any island nation would be viewed as completely normal.

Everything Ratu Vunni said tracked perfectly with Vela's version the night before. Dell was hoping this would be the case.

"How will we communicate?" asked Dell. "I'm in America most of the time and a single parent to a daughter I adore. I may not always be immediately available."

Vunni responded that the nature of Derek's assignments would be planned well in advance, allowing for Derek's personal life to be accommodated. "We use FAX machines to communicate," said Vunni. "You should have one at your home in California," he added. Dell said he not only had one at his house, he had one for his car, too.

The day progressed and Vunni politely answered Derek's numerous questions. Payment was the last subject covered. Again Vela's statements were confirmed. The amount of payment, travel expenses and other costs would be wire transferred to Derek's account of preference, anywhere in the world.

The meeting ended on a very enthusiastic note. Derek's handshake with Ratu Vunni signaled that they had a business arrangement but more importantly, a new friendship. Derek's ass was fractured from sitting on the hard floor for hours. This was always the case in Sevu Sevu. He never got used to it.

Vela invited Derek to meet his wife and children. Derek was honored. Vela's wife Marinea would have lunch prepared. As they wandered through the village Derek could again feel the eyes of all watching him. Marinea was poised in front of the bure with her baby daughter Milea in her arms. Her lovely Fijian smile greeted Dell with warmth. Peeking shyly around the corner of the structure was Vela's son Aquila. Lunch consisted of ikavakalolo (fish caught that day), rau rau and fruit. The beverage was tea.

Marinea was reserved and timid around Derek. This did not surprise Dell. He never understood why some people acted so shyly around him. Dell sensed she questioned whether he was the best choice for this type of work. It was important to Derek that he had Marinea's confidence. He wanted her to believe her husband was working with a safe partner. It was likely this would take time. Lunch concluded. Vela and Derek said their goodbyes and headed for the dock.

On the return trip downriver Vela and Dell were both excited over the events of the day. Vela needed this opportunity to support his growing family. Derek pondered many positive scenarios for his end of the work. Time passed quickly on the trip downstream.

After the dive operators' meeting concluded Derek Dell headed back to California. Though the meeting at Pacific Harbor provided direction for the coup-suffering dive industry, the meeting in the highland village of Maleqa would change the direction of Derek Dell's life.

Uncle Rico and 70 Wylvale

The long journey to California offered much time to think. Derek arrived in San Francisco even more enthusiastic than he was in Fiji.

Residual to his divorce was the disposition of the giant house he and Ann had built. He was delighted to discover a couple of good offers.

The house sold, Ann moved to LA and Derek set out to find a new home. He was looking for a place in Moss Beach on the west side of Highway 1, insisting on a location close to the ocean. One of Derek's good friends was a realtor.

Red Davis was not only a good friend but an accomplished professional who was certain to find Derek his ideal home. Derek, Town and Red were pals who had shared the type of relationship men value over long periods of their lives. The three got together as much as possible but Derek's extended trips overseas made scheduling difficult.

One day the phone rang. It was Red. In his relaxed, friendly style he explained to Derek that there was a small housing development on the location of the old Dan's Motel. During the years of prohibition Moss Beach was a liquor-smuggling drop. It was a town with a colorful history. The old motel acted as housing for the truck drivers who would transport the hooch up Highway 1 to San Francisco speakeasies.

The liquor drop zone was now the Fitzgerald Marine Reserve. The new houses were few, luxurious and sized perfectly for Derek. The west side location offered direct access to the beach and bluffs of the area. Derek, Lydia and their dog Franco could easily find happiness in this location. The house was on a cul-de-sac with only two other homes. The privacy and safety of tiny Wylvale Ave would suit their needs perfectly. Derek bought the house.

Close to the San Francisco Airport the Wylvale house became the launch point for Dell's travel needs and a unique setting in which to raise Lydia. It was a home cherished by Derek because his California life was the connection to normality that, over time, became vital for Dell's survival. As expected, Red Davis had found Derek his perfect home.

Derek received a FAX from Italy. Derek and Lydia were proud to be both Italian and American citizens. They traveled to Italy as often as possible, as Derek thought connecting Lydia to their family in Europe was important. The FAX was from Derek's uncle, Federico Pasceta in San Valentino, Italy. Everyone in the family simply called him Rico. Uncle Rico was Derek's favorite family member in Italy (though he never let that out). Rico was in his late 60s, handsome and very debonair. He sported a rich full head of beautiful gray hair and was slim and fit. Rico was always well dressed and fashionable. Even his casual attire was stylish, reflected a sense of color and coordination.

He said in the FAX he was retiring from his work in Italy and moving to San Francisco. He wondered if Derek could help with the relocation. Rico had a successful construction company and had sold it for a tidy profit. He had cash to buy a home in the city.

Derek approached Red Davis to find Rico a place. Red was the ideal answer to Rico's need. This would be fun. Not only would Derek have a ball spending Uncle Rico's money, but he could see to it the residence had two bedrooms. Who wouldn't want a place to occasionally spend a night in the city?

Red and Derek did exactly that. The search involved several outings in the North Beach area of San Francisco. North Beach is the Italian neighborhood of the city and would offer Rico a taste of home. This might assist in his transition. Rico was an accomplished gentleman with a colorful background. Nonetheless, he was getting older and Derek wanted to make his uncle's move to America as trouble-free as possible.

Searching for just the right property in North Beach was a ceremonious process for Red and Derek. It required several culinary episodes punctuated by broad samplings of wine. The boys believed Rico needed access to quality levels of both. Since Derek already knew the best places in the area, the research was more about confirmation than discovery. Both Red and Derek were committed to the challenge, particularly the quest for the perfect wine.

After two weeks of diligent effort, Red produced a

property he had found on the second day of their search. It was in the 1800 block of Grant St. The two-bedroom flat was right in Rico's price range. Most important, there was a garage. Uncle Rico drove a Maserati and would insist on cover. After a mountain of overseas phone calls, FAXs and wire transfers, the property was purchased and Uncle Rico had a new home in America.

Derek Sets Up

1989 could not have opened on a higher note. Derek and Lydia had the perfect home and so did Uncle Rico. Derek's new friendship with Vela would surely produce extreme diving experiences and some pretty good cash: two things required by Derek. It occurred to him that he may have found his yin and yang: the delicate balance of a normal life in California and one of high adventure in the South Pacific.

Uncle Rico was arriving today. Toddler Lydia and Derek waited outside customs at San Francisco Airport. After what seemed like forever, the doors swung open and the travelers began to appear. Only two people were ahead of Rico. Lydia had never met him but she smiled joyfully as he turned the corner. Likely she picked up on her dad's excitement. Rico didn't even look tired. With a spring in his step he dashed to Derek and Lydia. The greeting was typically Italian, with an embrace and kisses on both cheeks. He hoisted Lydia into his arms for a kiss and a loving hug. She warmed to Rico instantly.

The three struggled through baggage claim, loaded the car and headed toward Moss Beach. Rico planned on staying with Derek and Lydia until his furniture and belongings arrived from Italy. Of substantially more importance to Rico would be the arrival of his Maserati.

Derek and Rico were sports car guys. Rico had been a racing driver and succeeded where Derek had failed. Rico said, "Derek, you know, I am so excited to be living in California with-a you. It is a dream come true. Hey," he continued, "I love dis Chevy Tahoe. It holds so much. But I cannot wait to see your De Tomaso." Derek had two cars. The Chevy Tahoe did the daily work. Derek's pride and joy was his De Tomaso Pantera. One of few made, his was bright red with stylish tan leather interior. Alejandro De Tomasso was an experienced designer who struck out from Ferrari to build his own Italian supercar. The result was the Pantera. Derek had boosted the horsepower on his and refurbished the car with luxurious materials considered too expensive for the original machine. Uncle Rico had never seen a Pantera, let alone one with this opulence.

The drive from the airport to Moss Beach is spectacular. Highway 1 takes you over Devil's Slide, offering some of the most amazing ocean vistas imaginable. Rico was slack-jawed. Driving south toward Moss Beach, their Chevy exited the Slide and rolled down to Montara Beach. Mile-long sandy mounds were bracketed by rock outcropping at both ends of the beach. The underwater geography at Montara made it one of Derek's favorite surf spots.

A mile later Derek turns off Highway 1 and rounds the corner toward the ocean and Wylvale Ave. Rico is beaming with excitement. He loves the house and vows to visit as often as he can. "My Maserati and-a your Pantera park in the driveway will look like the start of-a Le Mans," Rico joked.

Franco the dog was simply delighted to have company. Rico was another pal who could take him for walks on the bluffs and beaches. Moss Beach was heaven for a dog. Dogs were heaven for Derek and Lydia. Rico seemed to have the same family gene, the one that endeared them to any animal they met.

The day ended early. Rico was feeling a little jet lagged and Lydia would want to retire early. They decided to adjourn to Mezza Luna Restaurant in the nearby harbor for an early dinner. Derek thought Rico would enjoy some authentic cuisine and Lydia loved the place. During dinner Rico asked how long it would take to drive to the flat in North Beach from the house. Derek suggested about forty-five minutes but, perhaps, less in the Maserati. Rico was already scheduling visits in his mind. He envisioned the Maserati howling over Devil's Slide.

Rico spoke in Italian to the waiter at Mezza Luna. It made them both feel at home. The owner overheard the conversation then visited the table to welcome a fellow countryman. Rico made the wine selection. They would drink only enough to enjoy the meal and assist with a comfortable sleep.

After an exceptional dinner the trio returned home. Rico was staying in Derek's office which doubled as a guest room. The FAX machine in the office was receiving an incoming communication. It was from Vela.

The Great Tonga Trench

The FAX directed date and destination. Derek was heading to Tonga. This was their first job. He would fly to Nadi, Fiji then on to Fua'amotu Airport in Tonga. The problem was, he had to leave in one week. Organizing his gear, flights and logistics would be easy compared to the larger question: who would look after Lydia? Ann was in Europe and Derek didn't even know exactly where she was.

There was a simple answer. Perhaps the closest Derek Dell ever got to having a sister was his friend Meg Page. Meg was Lydia's godmother and a friend of Ann's too. She was from an East Coast family. Well-heeled, they ensured Meg's education, both academic and social. Meg was single and loved her goddaughter immensely. She had the time to be an active part of Lydia's life. Meg often hosted events for Lydia and her friends and everyone was grateful for the loving care she offered. Meg was the perfect answer to Derek's dilemma.

Balancing his life as a dedicated single father and his duties in business was challenging for Derek. He knew, however, that the same challenges were faced by millions of single parents. No matter how different their work might be, single parents shared one common problem. They had to figure out a way to manage.

A week later Rico drove Derek to the airport. Derek was unusually quiet. Rico could tell Derek's mind was elsewhere. He asked if Derek was doing shark work this trip. Derek responded, "I do shark work on every trip, Uncle Rico. That's what the guest divers want to see."

Rico looked worried. He said, "You know, Derek, I knew a racing driver once. His name Zaffuto. Zaffuto say if-a you want to win-a da race, you *never touch-a da brake*."_Zaffuto lived his life by the same philosophy he used to drive the race car. Derek was curious as to why Rico told the story of Zaffuto. Rico said, "I worry dat-a you live like-a Zaffuto. I don't want you to crash like-a Zaffuto." Derek understood now. This was Rico simply saying he loved Derek and wanted him safe.

Vela greeted Derek as he exited Customs/Immigration at the airport in Tonga. Dell's trip down had been the usual litany of complications, moving mounds of dive gear and camera equipment halfway around the planet. The two loaded the luggage into a truck Vela had organized. The nitrox tanks were lodged against the truck-bed walls. They looked like any other scuba tank, only they had a chalk mark reading 36%. Off they went to the marina.

They boarded a fishing boat called the *Suzy Flounder*. Derek did not want to know how the name came about. It smelled like a fishing boat, of course, but Derek had hoped for a little more cleanliness. There were only the captain and one crew member. The captain was never called by name. The crew member was introduced as Frankie. This kid was fit and clearly well trained. He handled his job directly and with confidence. He appeared to be Tongan and his real name certainly was not Frankie.

Derek was fine with the secret nature of the work. He was, however, concerned with the secrecy of the captain and Frankie. It seemed that the crew should be open with one another. After all, they were all on the same team and out to complete the same job. Vela reminded Derek that the Ivy Bells divers and crew of the *Halibut* had no idea of the destination or details. Everyone understood the confidentiality of the information. "What's that got to do with us?" Dell asked.

"Nothing directly," replied Vela. "It is just the way military people are trained." Though Derek did not understand all the cloak and dagger, he accepted that the others were military trained and he was not.

On the three-hour trip to the dive site there was little said by the captain and Frankie. This did not help with Derek's confidence in his Tongan hosts. In the end, it was Vela who would be on the dive. Dell trusted Vela.

Derek and Vela geared up and splashed down. This was a mostly a blue-water dive and heading to a depth of two hundred forty-six feet. Derek had never dived that deep in his entire career. He found nitrox to be simply magic. He was so energized by the high oxygen content that the sluggishness of jet lag was completely absent. Vela carefully observed Dell's descent. Derek did the same with Vela.

The two gained instant confidence in one another as technical scuba divers. You could always tell. Neither man needed to look at their equipment to make adjustments. Clearing their ears during descent was effortless. One of the signs of a real pro in any activity is that they make it look easy. Such was the case as Vela and Derek dropped down to depth. They would be great partners.

As a diver descends, the working sound of the regulator differs. From the sound alone, Derek knew they had exceeded one hundred seventy-five feet. The bright sunlight from above was disappearing and the water darkened quickly.

A blue-water dive offers no visual landmarks to assist in your orientation. There are no reefs or floors so a diver can easily become disoriented and not even know the way up. Derek had preached for years: Panic equals death in the ocean. A warmth of concern began to invade his body. He remembered his mantra and quickly overcame the flash of anxiety. Vela never noticed.

Finally they reached the floor. Derek's depth gauge read two hundred forty-five feet. They swam to the hydrophones that were only a few meters away from where they bottomed out. The captain had put the boat directly on the job site. Derek was carrying a camera and strobe light but was not permitted to bring film. The cameras were just for show. No photographs were to be taken of the hydrophones or surrounding area.

Vela swiftly moved from one phone to the next checking for solid anchors, degree of encrustation and other issues that plague metal in deep salt water. Dell swam to the opposite end of the string of hydrophones and began the same process. The two would meet in the center.

The examination process was not materially different from the dive boat mooring inspections Aqua Trek did on dive sites. Dell was very comfortable with the entire process. Time was the critical issue on this dive. Even with nitrox the divers were very limited in their bottom time.

They completed their inspection and maintenance well within the time restraints. Derek thought that the humpback whale migration through Tongan waters this year would be well documented by the audio messages from the hydrophones.

Derek was overtaken by his well-known sense of humor. Of course, most Fijian people also have a highly developed sense of humor. This often generated unscheduled comedic moments. He simply could not resist.

Demonstrating unusual flipper and buoyancy control Derek began doing the Twist, Chubby Checker style. He popped the regulator out of his mouth and sang into the hydrophone. A bubbly verse completed,

Dell reconnected with Vela, who also twisted a couple of times and gave Derek the high five. The salute was created. After every dive they finished the guys would meet, twist twice and hit the high five. Vela and Derek were now a team.

The two ascended slowly. The process required decompression stops. The divers would spend time in the shallows, motionlessly stationed at twenty feet. Any bubble trouble that could develop from such a deep dive would subside at the decompression stop. Derek checked his dive watch, looked at Vela, nodded and headed to the surface.

The captain and Frankie assisted in getting the two divers back on the boat. *Suzy Flounder* was a fishing boat and not equipped with diver entry decks. After divesting themselves of tanks and weight belts, Derek and Vela kicked up to grasp the gunnels. It was an athletic effort indeed but Vela and Derek made it look easy.

The two debriefed the dive. Dell was enthusiastic about nitrox. He commented, "With that stuff I didn't even need my A game." Vela smiled. The long ride back to port allowed Derek to sleep. He needed lots of that.

On his way to slumber, he thought of the money. Dell hit the American Express card pretty hard. First class air, expensive everything. He was being reimbursed for those costs by whoever the hell he was actually working for, along with five thousand for the dive itself. He estimated about fifteen or twenty thousand dollars for a final tab.

Now the good part. Derek would have Aqua Trek pay his expenses as he usually did. That meant the wire transfer from Ratu Vunni could, in its entirety, sit offshore from the US in Derek's overseas account. This scheme tripled his profits from each outing with Vela. Even on a stinking fishing boat, Derek slept well on the ride to port.

Vela and Derek checked into an airport hotel for the night. It would be twenty-four hours before they could fly due to decompression requirements that follow a deep dive. They kept a low profile but did not try to hide from the public. After all, an underwater photographer like Derek would not raise an eyebrow ashore in Tonga. At dinner that night Vela suggested that the next dive would be the tiny South Pacific nation of Kiribati.

A Shift in Priorities

On arrival in Fiji, Derek and Vela went their separate ways. Dell would be doing Aqua Trek work for a week and Vela headed home to Maleqa and his family. They agreed to meet before Dell left for California.

Dell checked into the Regent as usual when he was in the Nadi area. He decided to have a quiet night and do the paperwork necessary to get paid. Feeling somewhat energized over the event, Derek was beaming as he figured the revenue after all expenses were added up. If he could do four or five of these dives per year, he could bank a tidy sum.

As the week went on Derek spent every day working with the Aqua Trek staff on Mana and in the Nadi office. People tend to think that anyone in the tourist business in an exotic destination like Fiji lives a life of leisure and relaxation. Simply not true. Aqua Trek business always included seeing accountants, lawyers and a number of government officials. As managing director, Derek was the person who carried those responsibilities. This was the part of business that Derek did not like. The accountants, lawyers and government officials didn't make things easier, they usually made them more difficult, and always more expensive.

Three days before Derek was scheduled to leave for California, he received a call from Vela. He wanted to meet at Derek's hotel the next day. Vela said he would be accompanied by a New Zealand SIS manager named Jenson Headman. "What does SIS stand for?" Dell inquired.

Vela said SIS stood for Security Intelligence Service. "Mr. Headman wants to discuss another diving job for us."

Dell was a little uncomfortable with this meeting. It just seemed too mysterious for his taste. He had no experience with people like Headman. They were spies and manipulators. Derek feared he could get in over his head pretty easy. Dell continued to rely on his trust in Vela. Their friendship was blossoming after the Tonga dive. In addition to his trust in Vela, Derek took another look at the revenue from the Tonga gig. The meeting was enthusiastically set for the next day.

Derek awaited his guests near reception at the Regent. A taxi rolled up and the two passengers entered the hotel lobby, eyes darting about, looking for Dell. Derek waved and the three men connected. Jenson Headman was an unfit, repulsive-looking man. Headman looked even more vulgar standing with an athletic Fijian like Vela. Introductions were made and they headed to the bar.

When Jenson Headman began to speak Derek was quite surprised. Despite his appearance, Headman was well versed in diving techniques and protocols. Could it be possible that this guy was an actual technical diver? As the conversation moved on Dell discovered that Jenson was not even a certified sport diver. He was, however, an intellectual of high order. Dell respected smart people.

The guys moved from the bar to the restaurant for lunch. Dell was more impressed as the meal progressed. Jenson spoke in detail about nitrox, deep diving, travel and logistical issues. Derek was now in awe of the knowledge Headman possessed on subjects he had never experienced. Perhaps that is why he was a manager.

After lunch they reconvened in the bar for coffee. The bar was near empty but Jenson led the men to a corner table, away from the entrance. Headman began by telling Derek he was impressed with his performance on the Tonga dive. Vela had briefed him. Dell was gracious but more interested in the next dive.

Jenson asked if Derek knew anything about Russian trawlers. Derek replied that he did not: however, it was common knowledge that the trawlers were all spy ships. Fishing was just a cover activity. Jenson was impressed with Dell's insight. Derek replied that trawler stories were on the news from time to time in California. Russian trawlers being spy ships wasn't much of a secret. "What does this have to do with our next dive?" Dell asked.

Jenson's voice lowered and Derek leaned in to hear better. Jenson said that the real threat posed by Russian trawlers was twofold. First, they engage in fishing treaties with developing South Pacific nations.

Kiribati and Vanuatu had both signed fishing treaties with the Russians. Fishing is very important to the economies of small island nations so the Russians gain great political power through the money they invest. "This is what you Americans call "the camel getting his nose under the tent," Jenson said. The problem was obvious. If the Russians gained favor with these tiny countries, they could negotiate for military bases being located there. "Like they did in Cuba?" Derek asked.

"Yes, just like Cuba," replied Jenson.

The issue was easy to understand but it seemed to Derek that politicians and diplomats were the people best equipped to address solutions. How does a simple scuba diver fit in? Jenson agreed that the first problem posed by Russian trawler activities had no place for divers. It was the second problem where diver came in.

Jenson next spoke of their concern about suitcase bombs. Derek asked what they were. Jenson explained that a suitcase bomb was a small amount of nuclear material contained in a package no larger than the average suitcase. If detonated in a city like Sydney or Auckland the damage could be horrific. Thousands would die. Their worry was a scenario where a Russian trawler could act as a suitcase bomb delivery vessel, disguised as a fishing vessel.

Dell said he thought that the Cold War was over after President Reagan gave the "tear down that wall" speech in Berlin. Russia was taking a position of detente. It was all over the news in the States. Jenson broke into laughter at the naivety of Dell's statement. Jenson informed Derek that the Cold War was in no way over and that spy activity would likely increase. It was clear that no-one trusted the Russian outreach by Gorbachev to Reagan.

"Still don't understand where diving comes in," stated Dell. Jenson explained that American satellite technology was able to detect nuclear material in large quantities. Satellite technology was at the core of America's Star Wars defense system. Dell had heard of that on the news as well. Satellite technology could not, however, detect the minute levels of nuclear material used for a suitcase bomb. "Those damn trawlers could be delivery systems for suitcase bombs," said Headman, sounding worried.

Jenson made it plain and clear. The divers would approach a trawler from beneath coming no closer than two hundred feet. They would carry equipment necessary to detect the small levels of nuclear material a suitcase bomb would contain. After taking a reading they would surface and head back. On its face it seemed pretty easy.

The meeting adjourned with Vela and Derek agreeing to meet the next day to plan logistics for the type of dive Jenson Headman had requested. Dell hated shaking hands with Headman. Jenson was a slimy bastard.

A Perfect Dive Strategy

The next morning Vela met Derek at the Regent for breakfast. The room was not crowded, it was early. Both Vela and Derek were early risers. The hotel laid out a startling buffet. Six types of juice, table after table of fruits, yogurt, cereal, eggs and omelettes, made any way you like, breads, muffins and on. The entire presentation sat amongst tropical flowers and plants. It made you instantly hungry.

The two moved around the room, selecting the right combination of delights for the first plate. Vela's appetite was always in gear. Dell was not really thinking about food.

They sat in a corner table, away from the growing activity at the buffet. Vela asked if Derek had questions. He did. Derek wanted to know what the status was. By that, he meant, would they be doing anything criminal? Vela assured Dell that swimming two hundred feet away from any boat violated no maritime laws. There was no military connection, they were not spies, and there was no violence. The divers would simply be acting like a safety officer at the airport. "The people who check your luggage for guns or bombs," Vela stated. Vela did say there were some rules.

The first rule was that they could not get caught with the reading devices or the nitrox regulators and tanks. It was technology that would be unexplainable and was of value to the Russians. That was easily resolved by just dumping their gear in the sea. Money seemed to be no object in the breakfast conversation.

Derek did not know what to call the technology. It sniffed out nuclear material but was not a Geiger counter. Dell suggested they call it a Karl Malden. Vela inquired, "What is a karlmalden?"

Dell replied that a Karl Malden was a he. Malden was an actor in *The Streets of San Francisco*, a television cop show of the 1970s running in the States. He was known for his giant nose and sniffed out crime with his partner Michael Douglas. The guys agreed on the name.

The next rule was a little sensitive. Vela spoke of the larger picture. Diving specifics were set aside while Vela discussed the politics of a job like this. Because they were not military, if they were caught nearly any mindless excuse could be offered for their presence near a trawler. Sport divers who drift away from their group; scientists getting lost and seeking help from passing boats; any nonsense would work. This was, in fact, the same type of phony notion that Russian trawlers were merely fishing. As long as the divers were not caught with a karlmalden or military tech regulators and tanks, any line would work.

The next problem they had to solve was the diver delivery method.

Suspect trawlers were tracked by all the countries Ratu Vunni hired out to. The divers could have relatively short notice on travel and possible long-range locations. This meant a long-range seaplane was required. Now, a seaplane was a piece of technology they really couldn't get caught with. Vela said, "If there is trouble the pilot will be instructed to fly off."

"Just leave us there?" Dell grimaced.

"We would be okay," Vela replied. "The Russians would use the event as propaganda, claiming to be heroes for saving poor lost divers."

The guys decided the best ploy was to simply not get caught, ever!

The critical element of dive strategy was getting from the plane to the trawlers. Dell's eyes grew large and excited. "WE NEED A ZODIAC!" Dell exclaimed. Vela responded that they surely did. Dell had spoken to Vela about the fun he and Town had on the waves of Northern California in the *Maniac*. Now, it appeared there would be another *Maniac* in the South Pacific. Dell loved the notion of naming their Zodiac *Maniac 2*. So did Vela. It seems to connect him to Derek's life in the States.

The dive itself would be nitrox, of course, and deep. The plan was to take the reading below two hundred feet and swim off horizontally, gently ascending. The bubbles from their regulators would take so long to surface that the divers would be long gone before they were noticed. They agreed the dive should be made pre-dawn. Darkness would be good cover and the sea would become active as morning feeding commenced. More good cover. The bottom time would be short and the entire dive would be less than twenty minutes. Still, the seaplane could not fly over one thousand feet on the trip back. This was a problem the guys thought should be discussed with that New Zealand butt blister, Jenson Headman. They finished eating then went to Derek's room to make some phone calls.

Dell decided to extend his stay. He ordinarily did not like to do this as he thought it upset Lydia. She never complained though. A call to the States and Lydia would be in the loving care of Meg for a little longer. Rico would handle the Moss Beach house and beloved dog Franco. All was well with Dell's extended stay. Besides, they still had to discuss the money. This gig would have a higher pay day after calling Headman. A meeting was set for the next day. He was bringing a pilot with him. This fellow would be an important member of the team. Both Vela and Derek needed to be comfortable with him. Vela felt it would be important to ask Ratu Vunni to attend. Dell agreed and organized a private conference room with the hotel concierge. Both men were anticipating finalizing the details for the first dive. If Derek was going to extend his stay, there needed to be a good reason.

It was nearing midday and Vela left to make further arrangements. Derek was heading to the pool to relax with a Fiji Gold or two.

The Kiribati Project

Derek slept like a baby that night. Feeling comfortable and safe allowed high levels deep R.E.M. slumber. The rituals Derek developed for post-dive relaxation were important to him. So were the various other habits he engaged in. Balance was key to coping with his complex life so he usually made time for himself.

Everyone was arriving for the meeting at ten a.m. After hitting the breakfast buffet Derek walked over to the hotel conference center to ensure the private room was stocked with water and coffee. Not only had they covered the basics, but an impressive layout of sliced fruit and baked goods was included. "Very upscale," Derek thought. He moved to the lobby and waited for the guys to show.

Punctuality was important to Derek Dell. He considered his and anyone else's time a most precious asset. Unfortunately, Fiji in general had no such concern over time. Derek had learned to cope and defined this lethargy as part of the charm of the place. To Dell's surprise the four men arrived exactly at ten a.m.

Derek greeted them with a smile. He was particularly glad to see Ratu Vunni. Jenson introduced Derek to David Paxton. David was the pilot who would ferry Vela and Derek to Kiribati. The five set out for the conference room.

Vunni took the lead when discussions commenced. Derek was a bit surprised as he expected Jenson to chair the meeting. The first subject was the aircraft. This would be an expensive element of the project so future use had to be discussed. Derek inquired, "What future use are you thinking of?" Vunni replied that Russian trawlers were everywhere. If the Kiribati project was successful, affordable and sustainable it would be repeated in other South Pacific locations.

Vunni insisted on a template strategy that would adjust as necessary when repeated. "This will allow for a greater front-end investment. That means more safety for you," Vunni offered.

Derek was now very surprised. Was Vunni Harvard Business too? The Ratu was obviously extremely smart, very experienced and knew his talent network and resources well. They were not just planning Kiribati, they were planning the entire 1990s.

The plane was David Paxton's area of expertise. Dave was a starched-collar Australian, every bit military. Paxton said, "You know, Derek, I saw you play baseball once on a video tape. They threw you out of the game! We are all military trained and these projects require strict disciplines. You don't seem to do well with rules. Will you be a risk, mate?"

"David," Dell replied, "I'm in my 40s, a single parent and running two businesses in different hemispheres. My life is all about personal discipline." Paxton seemed to accept that. Dell understood the question. After all, he was not military and his baseball style seemed to follow him around the world like a bad smell.

Paxton continued. The plane was to be a long-range seaplane, modified as needed to accommodate boat entry. It would have Fiji registry. He had decided on a GAF Nomad. It was an Australian plane that was now out of production. Dell knew nothing of aircraft but could see that money was no apparent object. Planning refueling stops and other transit support was discussed. It was all routine for Vunni. His network was everywhere. The matter of greatest concern was David Paxton's orders to abandon the divers in the event of trouble. Dell was squeamish at the notion of being left for dead.

Jenson Headman now spoke up. He confessed that the cold part of the Cold War with the Russians made this rule implicit. Getting caught red-handed (if you will excuse the pun) with military-only equipment could be seen as an act of aggression or otherwise politicized to the detriment of the West. "Without the karlmaldens, the nitrox rigs and the plane, you guys can get away with nearly any ridiculous explanation. That is also the cold part of the Cold War. We're allowed to bullshit each other." Dell thought that if your eyes could struggle past Headman's disgusting appearance, you found he was smart and experienced. Derek decided to use the situation as a negotiating point for more pay.

Ratu Vunni re-took the lead. He explained that our nitrox regulators would be sent to us along with an oxygen analyzer. The equipment would be delivered by DHL to Moss Beach. Confidentiality of even its existence was critical. Derek was to personally maintain the gear and oxygen scrub the device for nitrox use. It should be locked away and always in his custody. When in the field it was his job to test the air in the tanks to ensure it was 36%. That was the reason for the oxygen analyzer. The redundancy and responsibility systems were for safety and often used in technical diving.

Essentially, Ratu Vunni was using diplomatic pouch rules to allow DHL to pass through customs in Fiji and the USA without a contents search. Dell was feeling out-and-out scared by the power these guys were wielding. He did not want that to show.

Vunni turned to Derek for the next issue. "Derek, you are the expert on the next matter," said Vunni. "Tell us what you need in a boat."

Derek Dell was now in control of the meeting. Having heard the others ease into the notion of repeat projects after Kiribati, Derek decided to speak directly to the matter.

He began, "This business of "leave ya dead, Dave" over here, flying off if trouble develops, is our weak spot. No sense in setting up a future gig if old Dead Dave leaves us for, well, dead." In Derek's unmistakably American style, a new nickname had been hatched. Dead Dave was the only link between Vela and Derek being caught in a political mess or even worse. The *Maniac 2* was their link to Dead Dave.

Dell continued, "I want a thirteen-foot Zodiac, Lombard edition. Black, military-level Hypalon. Hard hull, muscular transom, aluminum floor, oversized pontoon and bow rigged to strap in heavy metal. I want a long-shaft 35 HP Yamaha, injection tricked to bump horsepower. Torque prop in case I have to rock that bitch out of the jungle. Secondary engine will be a bass boat electric. Of course, the biggest, fastest one possible. Everything about this boat needs to make it faster!"

"I actually only understood the last sentence, about speed," said Jenson. They agreed that Ratu Vunni would get the *Maniac's* specifications and obtain the craft. All were curious about the request for the electric engine. Dell offered, "Detection is not an option is it? Sound travels over water quite well. Dead Dave can land further away allowing for greater cloaking. The *Maniac* will deliver us even closer at high speed. To do the job quickly we want to minimize the swimming time. If the *Maniac* has a secondary soundless electric engine, we can cut our actual dive time substantially by getting even closer to the trawler, particularly in the dark."

This made sense to everyone. The ingredient that brought smiles to the faces of all was the fact that Derek demonstrated mission critical thinking. This was important to military people. Dell gained acceptance, even with Dead Dave.

The last item on the agenda was the most important to Derek. How much money would be paid? Ratu Vunni looked Derek in the eye so as to say there would be no negotiation. He stated, "You will be paid USD $20,000 per dive plus expenses." Derek immediately agreed since he was only looking for USD $10,000. This was unbelievable money. Derek could haul in around USD $50,000 every time he swam a karlmalden by a trawler. "Rack 'em up, baby," Derek thought.

The next day Derek Dell boarded the plane for California. His sun tan and smile said he was returning from vacation. That was the norm for Derek.

Song of the 90s
The Kiribati Template

Derek loved living in Moss Beach. It was his connection to normal life. His activities in the South Pacific could be shelved and his mind (and soul) could rest. Routines were established and rhythms set in. All of them pleasant, playing out against the back drop of the California coast. Derek and Lydia took Franco to the beach near the house daily. Lydia's mom had returned to San Francisco. This was good for his daughter. Derek wanted Lydia to have the convenience of mom and dad nearby.

Uncle Rico was frequently at the Moss Beach house. Having him in Lydia's life gave the family a sense of depth and roots in Italy. Rico and Derek became closer sharing a friendship reaching beyond their family ties.

Sundays were usually culinary experiences where Rico's considerable kitchen skills were passed along to Lydia and Derek. The very dapper Uncle Rico would ease up in his Maserati with bags abundantly full of ingredients.

The preparation process would take much of the day. The eating process, the remainder of the day. Each course punctuated by strolls to the beach with

Franco. Traditions like this were important to Derek and a sound foundation for Lydia.

It had become clear to Derek that the Tonga Trench hydrophone dive was merely a test. Jenson Headman did not seem like the kind of guy who gave a damn about the whales.

Dell's pay safely arrived in Cayman Island and he began to develop trust in the financial arrangement. Derek was anxious for the Kiribati dive and to refine the drawing-board template. This was the big money play.

The FAX machine in Derek's office set off. He was to be in Fiji in four weeks. Derek estimated the entire event would take around five days. He didn't need to organize for or to explain away more than a week's absence. That was a snap!

The routine was usually the same. Derek would arrive in Fiji and check into the Regent. Instead of the usual two days of relaxation, Vela would pick him up shortly after Dell dropped off his baggage. There was no leisure buffet breakfast, no lingering over coffee or any of his standard arrival rituals. It was straight to a warehouse in Lautoka.

Lautoka was a town located about twenty-six miles west from Nadi and the Regent hotel. It was a business center and industrial area. A very pleasant place in all. Vela stopped the truck near a warehouse and walked quickly with Derek to the entry.

Vela swung the large entry door open and revealed to Derek the subject of their drive. It was the *Maniac*

2. There she was. Jet black and brand new. Every detail of specifications Derek requested was included. Even the bow line length was correct. Dell needed to lash the line to his left arm while using his right to handle the engine tiller. This high-performance stance was the key to big wave maneuvering in the *Maniac*. The battery for the supplemental electric engine was located forward too. It was part of Derek's request that heavy gear be bow mounted.

With dive gear, Vela and the karlmaldens all set forward, this boat would balance out better than the original *Maniac* in California. The look on Derek's face said it all. The combination of joy, excitement and a slight hint of lust told a frightening story of what Derek Dell was going to do with that boat!

Vela and Derek were to meet Dead Dave at noon on a beach near the Nomad float plane. Vela and Derek towed the *Maniac* to an empty location away from town. They dragged the boat over the beach on its launch wheels. Once in the water Derek fired the engine. It started on the very first pull.

The *Maniac* handled just like the California original. Derek was delighted. He spied Dead Dave and the Nomad a few meters off his starboard bow.

Derek was surprised at the size of the Nomad. Much larger than he thought. Of more surprise was the gaping rear end slowly opening to receive the *Maniac* and two divers. The Nomad was old. Derek could tell even though he knew nothing of aircraft. That said, there was no doubt a small fortune was spent by that maggot larva Jenson Headman and his people, whoever they were.

From Fiji it was over two thousand miles to Kiribati. Vela and Derek settled in while Dead Dave earned his keep at the Nomad's helm. Derek carefully examined the dive gear and analyzed the air in the tanks. Everything was in perfect shape. The guys decided to chat. They were way too excited to sleep, read or listen to music. Conversation would ease their angst and deepen the friendship that was in blossom.

Conversations ranged from general topics on diving to very personal matters pals will discuss. These were the moments that bind. The tipping point where friendship turns into brotherhood. Derek could be completely open and truthful with Vela. Due to the secret nature of the work they shared, each had only the other to confide in. More importantly, each had only the other to trust. Though they trusted Dead Dave, the thing they could trust most about him was that he would follow orders and fly off leaving them to their own survival devices.

Vela asked, "Derek, how do you plan to deal with the secrets we must keep regarding our work?" "I have no real plan," said Derek. "I was just going to shut up." "That is not far off from the best plan," said Vela. "The most important point in keeping our stealth is to never lie. If you begin to lie you will not be able to remember the lies you have told. People will start to notice those inconsistencies over time." Derek had never thought about it before but Vela was absolutely correct. Derek could never remember a pack of lies. It was becoming more obvious that Derek was selected for this work partly because the actual functions of his diving career meshed perfectly with the needs of this project. Withholding information was much easier than lying. There was nothing to remember. This would be easy for a loner like Derek.

Vela asked, "Do you have a girlfriend Derek?" "No, not really," Dell replied. "Is that important?" "No," said Vela. "It is just that the Aqua Trek staff tells me you come to Fiji with different women many times. Mostly blonde-haired, big titted girls with long thin legs," Vela noted. Derek chuckled, "Those girls are models I work with in underwater photography. The long blonde hair shows well with the reds and blues of the soft corals. Aqua Trek is in the tourist business and pretty girls sell the product well." "Are they all your girl friends?" Vela inquired. "Some were," said Dell. "Being a single dad and business owner leaves little time for serious relationships," Dell lamented.

Vela continued. He was not prying into Derek's personal life he was leading up to a point. Just like his advice on lying, Vela had advice on relationships while doing this work. Vela recommended that, if Dell were not head over heels in love with a woman, he limited the time of the relationship. Dell asked "You mean like a statute of limitations in law?" "Yes," replied Vela. Though it depended on the girl, six months was the suggested time. After six months in a relationship, feelings begin to develop. Those feelings can lead to pillow talk. That might lead to Derek having to lie.

Lies cannot be remembered. For everyone's safety (including the girlfriend) Dell understood that limiting his time in a relationship was sound thinking.

Dead Dave flew the Nomad tirelessly. Fuel stops were closer to pit stops in Formula One racing. The support team Dead Dave had arranged was outstanding. The divers had no idea where they were and relied entirely on Dead Dave. Finally, the Nomad landed in open water.

The sea was calm. The rear of the Nomad opened and the *Maniac* was deposited in the ocean. The boys wore black surfing wet suits that allowed for better shoulder motion. With gear properly loaded forward they set out for the lights of the fishing boats lining the horizon.

In the darkness it would be hard to tell which boat was the Russian trawler they were to read. Vela acted as navigator and Dell trusted him to sight the proper craft.

Due to the flat water and quiet night Derek kicked in the electric engine long before needed. Visually cloaked in darkness and silently cloaked with the electric engine Vela and Derek moved closer to the fleet.

Upon Vela's signal Derek stopped the *Maniac* and gingerly eased the anchor into the bottomless ocean. There was no buoy or floor to anchor on. The anchor weight left dangling in blue water would only serve to minimize the *Maniac*'s motion while the divers swam off to read the trawler.

The boys slipped gently over the *Maniac*'s pontoons hardly disturbing a molecule as they entered the water. No gasp of air, hiss of a regulator test or any sound at all. Derek carried the karlmalden while Vela navigated from his dive computer. They dropped to two- hundred and forty-five feet.

There was no current and moonlight shone brightly in the water. The prism effect of water divided the shafts of moonlight making the entire scene appear to sparkle. With no land, reef or bottom anywhere nearby the luminescence of open water felt astral in nature.

Derek began to feel angst at depth like he did on the Tonga Trench dive. Fear and panic have one common enemy. FOCUS! Derek had experienced the creeping heat of fear many times while diving. Original shark wranglers were scared all the time. He knew if he concentrated on the mechanical functions and duties of the dive there would be no room for fear. No place for panic. Focus past your fear and angst will dissolve. This worked every time.

The divers settled in comfort at a depth of two-hundred and fifty feet. Swimming horizontally Vela lead them to the Russian boat. A reading was taken as Derek swept the length of the trawler. He used a camera motion designed for smooth panning with a video system. This was perfect for a karlmalden read as well.

They reversed their direction, stayed at depth and headed for the *Maniac*. As they increased their distance from the trawler, they gradually ascended. Vela navigated them to the *Maniac* flawlessly. Derek could see the silhouette of the *Maniac* against the moonlight as they swam toward the anchor. While they floated vertically at twenty feet enjoying a decompression stop, they faced one another, twisted twice and hit the high five. This was a salute to their second job.

It was a technical yet simple dive. Vela, Derek and Dead Dave flew back to Fiji confident that the template they had developed could be safely repeated in any South Pacific locale. The boys had discovered that their "Song of the 1990s." It would be the Kiribati template.

The California Girls

Arriving home in Moss Beach generally had form and structure. Another ritual that helped Dell refocus his life. The cleaning and stowing of dive and camera equipment signaled Derek that he was returning to his beloved normal. Then, of course, there was Lydia.

Nothing meant more to Derek that being Lydia's Dad. He took parenting very seriously and participated in every school event he could. Lydia was growing up and attending the Hamlin School in San Francisco. Hamlin was a private girls' school that required uniforms, offered a grand diversity of academics and schooled kids in social matters too. It was the perfect environment for Lydia to thrive.

Lydia and Derek's commute to the City each day took about forty minutes. They angled up Highway 1 traveling some of the most beautiful coastline in California. The time was never wasted. They sang songs, discussed pressing kid issues and told jokes.

They frequently picked up Lydia's friends and car pooled the city part of the drive. Derek loved his daughter's friends and tried to make the drive fun. They usually stopped at Enteman's Bakery on Van Ness. The car full of plaid dress girls loved the bakery bounty.

Lydia's friend Annie Nielsen was one of Derek's favorite kids. She was a blue-eyed blonde-haired darling that looked straight out of California's surfing culture. Lydia was a brown-eyed brown-haired version of the same California image. The girls' favorite commute song was the *California Girls* by the Beach Boys.

When Derek was about six or seven, he was developing an identity as an athlete. He thought it was good for young kids to identify with something positive even though interests might change as they grew older. Lydia and Annie became "The California Girls". They looked forward to the singing and bakery stops every day. So did Derek.

The California Girls could grow in numbers if there was a sleep over or other group activity. They were all California Girls when hanging out in Moss Beach.

As the 90s rolled on Derek and Lydia acquired two new family members. Eagle was a rescued race horse and Bucky a warm-hearted pony. The two were boarded at a nearby Moss Beach horse ranch. Having the ocean, horses and open space so close to San Francisco was heaven for Lydia and her pals. Moss Beach was a magnet for the city kids of The Hamlin School.

This was Derek's joy. The California Girls contributed to his grounding. Normal California living balanced his life. It was a stark contrast to his ventures into the abyss and secret jobs with Vela and

Dead Dave. Derek's need for normal and compelling need for adventure were both being answered.

Then there was the known work of Aqua Trek. Often a conversation point at school social events. Curiosity over Derek's shark-wrangling and the odd relationship with reinsurance activities at Triple C Re made him a subject of interest to other parents at The Hamlin School. Despite a crazy variance between California living and covert Russian trawler diving, things were working out pretty well for Derek Dell.

Uncle Rico continued to be a valued friend and family member. He schooled Derek in the finer things. Rico was a man of taste and experience. A perfect mentor for Derek. Rico loved cigars. Not a hard tobacco habit but the occasional enjoyment of an expensive hand-crafted Cuban. Good cigars were something they savored together.

He taught Derek the value of taking time for a simple thing like a good shave. Rico was an expert on shaving creams, razors and associated lotions. Sophistication provided by Rico was turning the baseball player into a gentleman.

Derek thought travel was an important part of Lydia's education. The two made frequent trips to Europe visiting Italian family and any number of museums and Cathedrals.

On other occasions God Mother Meg would escort the California Girls to Fiji meeting up with Derek after his work assignments were complete. No matter where the group went the kids enjoyed and learned from the travel experience.

The 1990s were not without their rough spots. In 1994 Franco died. The blow of losing their first dog was devastating to both Derek and Lydia. Derek's closeness to Franco was a staple of his grounding. Dell's life of secrecy and isolation was never lonely in part because of his community with animals. Franco's loss was staggering.

To deal with the pain of his passing Derek and Lydia acquired two new friends. Wylie was a fluffy white rescue dog mix hosting a good bit of arctic wolf. Marco was a brown and white high-end springer spaniel obtained from a breeder. They were both crafted by love and became close family additions.

Derek, Vela and Dead Dave scanned trawlers in several South Pacific locations. They encountered little in the way of problems and were profiting substantially from the work. Everything was going so well that Derek began feeling nervous over his success.

Over time Derek estimated that a small fortune was being spent on the Russian Trawler readings. This had to be more important work than Derek thought. The protocols of getting caught with equipment remained just plain scary to Derek. Paranoia was setting in.

Dell began to acquire weapons. He was certainly no hunter but enjoyed target and skeet shooting. Concern over personal vulnerability due to his special diving activities was offset by confidence his growing arsenal provided. At an intellectual level Derek knew that the powers of the West or the powers of Russia could eliminate him in an instant — weapons or not. The fact is, all that hard steel and a few thousand rounds of ammunition simply made him feel better.

The 90s were a time of great technical advancement. One critical to Derek was a Samsung cellular telephone with worldwide communication abilities. It was presented to him by Ratu Vunni. Derek was instructed to substitute the internal chip with one provided by the Ratu. Not only did the phone offer international communications, with Ratu Vunni's chip installed the phone provided SECURE international communications. Derek loved this toy. He used it to call Lydia from all over the world. He called it "Sammy".

The trawler diving rhythm continued through the decade. Off to Fiji, work with Aqua Trek, sneak off with Dead Dave and Vela, then back to California. Over and over again the routine was executed. Vanuatu, the Great Barrier Reef, New Guinea, everywhere the Russian trawlers sailed. The Kiribati template worked every time.

A strong brotherhood was developing between the three men. It stemmed from time on the job and mostly while airborne. Their conversations in the belly of the Nomad were its basis and the growing trust in one another was the glue.

Money was piling up in Cayman. A financial move had to be made. Dell was frequently under audit by the IRS. His foreign dive business caused him to be of interest to those guys. When Derek complained to Vela or that bridge troll Jensen Headman the IRS issues seemed to melt away never costing Derek a nickel. Though he never knew for sure, Derek believed his continued trawler work often got him out of the cross hairs of the IRS. Still, something had to be done and it had to satisfy the prying eyes of the Financial Feds.

The answer to that problem lay to the North.

The French Connection

It was the end of 1998. About two hours' drive north of San Francisco lies Mendocino County. Derek and Lydia decided they wanted a ranch of their own. A place to keep Eagle and Bucky. A place to experience the peace of mind and change of pace rural living can offer. Their research led them to Miracle Mountain Ranch in the tiny hamlet of Willits. The ranch was for sale.

The place was the perfect supplement to Moss Beach. MMR had extraordinary tactical design. It was forty acres in total. The housing area was located on top of a hill overlooking the pastures and barns below. Derek's escalating paranoia was soothed by the steep open ascent required to get near the house. With his volume of hardware and ammo he could defend that turf from nearly anything. Derek had a safe place.

Purchasing Miracle Mountain Ranch allowed Derek to bring funds onshore from his Cayman account, pay the requisite taxes and keep his money in real estate rather than a Cayman bank. Real estate is pretty cut and dried as far as the IRS is concerned. Derek thought this move would lessen their interest in him.

Setting up the ranch was a lot of work. He hired a

manager to mind the property when Derek was in Moss Beach or overseas. Her name was Nancy and she was an accomplished horsewoman. Derek felt the ranch was in very good hands and he could freely move around the world as needed. That comfort level came just in time. The Sammy was ringing.

No longer did Derek need the aging technology of a FAX machine to communicate with Ratu Vunnni, Jensen Headman, Dead Dave or Vela. The Sammy was great! Ratu Vunni's call was cordial but direct. Derek was instructed to report to Maleqa village in two weeks. Derek thought this to be a bit odd. Why Maleqa? The guys normally departed from Lautoka on the other side of the big island. Something important was up.

Derek arrived in Fiji on cue. Vela was not at the airport to greet him. He proceeded straight to the Regent with a heightened curiosity.

Derek was due at Pacific Harbor Resort in Beqa the next morning. He had an entire day to kill at the Regent.

After a trip to the fabulous buffet breakfast Derek decided to hit the pool, get some sun and sleep. He rounded the corner looking to find a lounge when his eyes fell upon a frightening sight. There lay Jensen Headman wearing a speedo men's bikini!

Dell could feel his meal surging up from his stomach toward his mouth. His hands became clammy and perspiration dotted his forehead.

Jensen's bleached blubber drooped over the

skimpy swimsuit making him appear naked. Derek's distress was a combination of what his eyes were seeing and what his mind was imagining. This was no way to deal with jet lag.

Derek greeted Jensen warmly. After all, there was good money on the table. Dell trusted Ratu Vunni, Vela and Dead Dave. He did not trust Jensen. The fact is, Derek was scared of Headman. He thought Jensen had power with the American IRS. That alone was chilling.

They filled the day with low level chit chat and spoke nothing of business. A couple beers together and Derek was softening his position on Headman. Jensen was a decent guy, he was simply stuck in a dirty job. Intelligence was surely dicey work, even in the South Pacific.

The following morning the two men climbed in Jensen's car and headed to Beqa. They arrived at a boat dock located at the mouth of the Nasouri River. It is near the capital city of Suva. Dead Dave and Vela were there with a Yamaha banana boat in hand. The four headed up the Nasouri for the long trip to Maleqa.

Vela provided sulus for Jensen, Dead Dave and Derek. There would be a Sevu Sevu in the village and traditional dress was important.

At Maleqa the four were directed to the Bure Kalou. Ratu Vunni joined the group and they all sat in a circle around the Tanoa. The Sevu Sevu began. The ceremony was taken seriously by all the men. Something told Derek this was no ordinary meeting and the subsequent dive was no ordinary gig.

With the ceremony completed, business commenced. Ratu Vunni told of a trawler that was headed toward French Polynesia. There was quite a difference when Tahiti was involved. French Polynesia was, essentially, part of Europe. The guys would be performing unauthorized work in a sovereign western country.

Though Ratu Vunni had people in French Polynesia the team would be working without the knowledge of the French Government. Of additional concern was a technical matter that was the reason a close-up trawler reading was critical.

For decades the French used the tiny atoll of Moruroa as a place to test nuclear weapons. Fishermen joked that the sea life in many nearby lagoons glowed in the dark. The protests were so prolific against this activity that the Green Peace ship Rainbow Warrior showed up to lend support. The ecological issue was a high-profile public struggle. Detecting a dirty bomb from a far could be tricky because of the blur of radiation Moruroa presented. Worse, an incident in Papeete would be considered an attack on the West. No one in the remote village bure even wanted to imagine what that could lead to.

When the meeting ended Derek and Vela walked to Vela's family bure. It was always good to see Marinea and the kids. Derek had become a family member in Baralavela household. This visit was brief as they had to head down river with Dead Dave and

Jensen. They ended by Derek promising, as always, to take good care of Vela. "After all, Marinea," Derek joked, "he owes me money."

On the trip down the Nasouri Dead Dave, Vela and Derek discussed the unique circumstances of this assignment. They agreed that the actual functions of the project would be the same as always. The Kiribati template had been perfected over the years and the team saw no reason to alter it further. The next day Dead Dave would fly the boys out of Lautoka as usual. The *Maniac* and the Nomad were readied.

On the long flight from Fiji to French Polynesia, Derek slept soundly. He only woke when the Nomad landed for fuel in the Cook Islands. Jet lag hit him pretty hard this trip. He overheard Dead Dave yelling at the fuel boat driver. There was a problem and a slight delay. Timing was important on these projects as the cover of darkness was necessary. The fuel delay caused all three men to worry.

Dead Dave flew franticly from the Cook Islands toward Tahiti. He wanted to make up time. Unlike the other assignments, Derek and Vela knew exactly where they were diving. The sensitive political issues required that they take special precautions in the event of discovery. A good story required them to know exactly where they were.

To Derek Dell's surprise the Nomad was landing just off the atoll of Rangiroa. Derek's face grew warm and he smiled from ear to ear. This was the home of the Avatoro Pass, the site of his first venture into shark-wrangling over fifteen years earlier. Derek wondered if Christophe was still alive.

There was no time to reminisce. The divers were worried about daylight. The rear of the Nomad opened and the *Maniac* slipped into the water.

The horizon was lit by the fishing boats outside the lagoon. There were only a few. The sun was beginning to rise and the sky brightened. Derek and Vela did not like this timing, not at all.

The trawler was easy to spot. It was the largest of the fishing craft in the area. Derek had killed the outboard and was switching to electric power when he heard the unmistakable whine of dual engines at full throttle. He raised his head and saw Vela dumping dive gear and both karlmaldens in the drink. In an instant Derek knew they were busted.

Next, they heard the Nomad fire and saw Dead Dave powering into the sky. Vela looked at Derek. His face said he did not know what to do next. One of the reasons Derek was hired for this project was his fast thinking and quick wit. He was the one who would flash that disarming smile and bullshit their way out of trouble.

The two divers saw three large military Zodiacs coming at them full speed from the Russian trawler. They were dual engine twenty-foot craft that were substantially faster than the *Maniac*. Both guys were certain that talking their way around this was not going to work. Vela said he was sure the Russians had seen the Nomad. This was a terrible mess.

The most dangerous place a man can arrive is at the three-way intersection of fear, adrenaline and testosterone. Derek and Vela sat clearly at that crossroads. They decided to run!

The *Maniac* instantly planed to full speed. Derek was so excited that while barking out instructions to Vela, he accidentally called him Town. This was no post-dive frolic in California with Town. These guys were running for their lives!

The Russians were gaining on the smaller *Maniac*. Derek could outmaneuver them but he didn't stand a chance in open water. The Russians could simply chase the *Maniac* until it was overtaken or ran out of gas. There was only one possibility. Derek advised Vela to hang on and balance in the bow of the *Maniac*. They were headed to the Avatoro Pass where the morning waves would be breaking big. Derek was taking the Russians into the jungle.

In his mind Dell thought there was no damn Russian who could stay with a California surfer in the jungle, even an average surfer like Derek. He was certain the torque prop and balance of the *Maniac* provided him and Vela with the upper hand. A surge of confidence overcame Derek as he leashed his left wrist to the bow line and hit the throttle.

South Pacific waves differ from California waves. The tropical versions are thinner than California swells. They tend to curl and tube while California waves mostly collapse. Derek had surfed them both.

As they approached the pass Derek saw his timing

was lucky. A pretty good-sized wave was rolling to its break point. One of the Russian boats was closely on the *Maniac's* tail. The two other veered off as they neared the waves.

The *Maniac* zoomed full speed off the backside top of the wave. They had to clear the jungle. This meant flight. Vela had to press forward toward the bow or the *Maniac* would flip backwards into the jungle. Vela was a better athlete than Town. His instincts and experience in the ocean were evident in the way he quickly balanced the *Maniac*. The guys were in the zone, totally in tune with the rhythm of the earth.

The *Maniac* flew level and landed in white water, well past the impact zone in the jungle. They lurched forward until Derek regained control of the tiller. He spun the boat around to see the fate of their Russian pursuers.

They spied the Russian Zodiac as it attempted to follow the *Maniac* through the air. Though Derek felt the Russians deserved an "A" for courage, he smirked as he watched the back-heavy Zodiac flip over in the surf line. Those powerful engines dragged the Russian craft under, depositing sailors everywhere.

"HOW YA LIKE THE JUNGLE, YOU FUCKING BORSHT-BELCHING BITCHES!" Derek yelled at the top of his lungs. Vela was in double shock. First there was the *Maniac's* flight. Second, as a military professional he would never trash-talk his opponent like that. An American baseball player, however, certainly would.

The second Russian Zodiac found its way around the surf line and entered the lagoon in pursuit of the *Maniac*. Derek and Vela were making a run for land. If they could escape into the island somewhere, Vunni might be able to get them safely out.

It became clear the Russians would overtake the *Maniac* long before land was reached. Derek and Vela did not know where the third Russian boat was but the second Zodiac was gaining on them and something had to change.

Derek reversed his direction and headed straight toward the surf line. The Russians did the same. Dell could see that the Avatoro Pass was breaking right and tubing. He had only surfed in the arched curl of a wave a couple of times in his entire life. To be entirely surrounded by a circle of water in the *Maniac* would likely end the Russian's pursuit. Their boat was simply too big and ponderous.

The *Maniac* hit the lip of the wave and veered left down the face. The torque prop grabbed when the *Maniac* cranked a bottom turn and blew into the tube. The boys were frozen still in awe. There was no need to move or balance. The natural power of the wave and the sweet spot position they were in made the tube ride pure circular joy. As the wave began to break Derek hit the power, flying off the shoulder into calmer waters. They turned to see how the Russians had fared.

Vela yelled and pointed off the stern. The big Zodiac had overturned and there were no signs of the sailors. The churning energy of tubing waves causes the "Maytag" effect. While the extraordinary buoyancy of the enormous Zodiac would pop it to the surface, the sailors would be dragged to the bottom and flushed out of the pass to waiting sharks. Vela stared into Dell's eyes. They both knew the sailors' fate. Poor guys didn't stand a chance.

The stakes had changed. People were now dead. This catastrophe had the potential of an embarrassing international incident. The Russians must have known the boys were coming. They were too well prepared. What the hell had happened? Derek thought. The two divers simply had to get away. Their focus turned toward the third Russian Zodiac.

The *Maniac* struggled through the surf line, straight toward an open water path through the lagoon. By now Dead Dave would have radioed Ratu Vunnni about the bust. Their best play was to hope that Vunni's network could help them out. The divers were making another run for shore.

The last Russian boat was nowhere in sight. Derek and Vela thought they might make land safely. Then from the port side of the *Maniac* Vela spotted the final Russian Zodiac. Not only was their boat faster, they had an easy angle of pursuit. The *Maniac* was in trouble.

Derek spun the *Maniac* and stopped dead in the water. He looked toward the surf line, seeking, at least, some hope. The tingling feel of desperation shot through his body. Vela yelled, "Bosso, we have to move now. We have to get away." Derek thought of Julia Pfeiffer State Beach. The day he and Town made the impossible jump over the Pacific Trench wave. A decision was made.

The *Maniac* revved to full speed. Dell and Vela shot straight at the Russian Zodiac. Derek yelled to Vela, "We're gonna jump the wave. When we hit the air, move way forward." Vela smiled and nodded in compliance. He had seen the pictures of the Julia Pfeiffer jump and knew exactly what Derek was going to do.

They nearly hit the Russians when they flew by toward the surf line. The powerful Russian boat spun and gave chase to the *Maniac*. Vela and Derek could see a large wave building. The *Maniac* remained at full speed.

Derek felt confident when the *Maniac* began to ascend the face of the massive wave. The torque prop was pounding. The Russians had the balls to follow. If they both cleared the crest of the wave Derek wasn't certain what the next move would be. He concentrated on the moment, focused past his fear.

The *Maniac* blasted toward the lip and the air above. From beneath, a surge of water hit its forward pontoons. The *Maniac* launched into the air. The lip of the wave flicked both boats skyward. The *Maniac* spiraled and landed dead in the jungle, upside down. The Russian boat simply flipped backward into the impact zone.

Derek and Vela were thrown from the boat into

the Avatoro's churning waters. Derek was leashed to the *Maniac* with the bow line. The water dragged him down, time and again. In each instance the left arm leash held. When the boat popped up, Derek could gasp a breath of air and ready himself for the next Maytag. Again he would be dragged down. Derek thought his wrist might rip apart from the pulling force of the Avatoro water. During a surface breath he moved the leash to his elbow for greater connection to the *Maniac*. It was his only hope.

On one surge underwater Derek was bumped by a Russian who was tumbling to the bottom of the passage. It scared Dell deeply as he watched the Russian flow downward to his death.

There was no sign of Vela. He was not leashed to the *Maniac*. Derek had not seen him underwater and feared his friend was lost. He scanned the surface franticly and peered into the eye-burning salt water, looking for any sign of Vela.

The wave set passed and Derek swam the inverted *Maniac* out of the jungle into calmer waters. He was exhausted, scared but alive and relatively well. His left wrist would never be the same.

He crawled on top of the *Maniac*, hoping to get a better view and sight Vela. He saw a couple of Russian sailors floating around. He could not tell if they were dead or alive but their life vests eventually popped them up. There was no sign of Vela. Emanueli Baralavela was dead.

Derek collapsed on the *Maniac* and broke into

tears. Vela was not coming up. Vela was dead. Derek thought of Marinea and the children. Oh, God, what had he done? His guilt and pain were staggering. Dell wanted to die.

Wanted, Dead or Alive

Derek Dell lay defeated on the inverted *Maniac* for nearly a half hour, by his guess. A helicopter appeared on the horizon and was heading directly toward him. It hovered over the *Maniac* while a rescue diver was lowered. Derek was harnessed and hoisted to the opening in the helo. The rescue diver descended back toward the *Maniac* and drew a massive knife. He slashed the *Maniac*'s pontoons and Derek watched it sink. Not only had Derek lost Vela, the *Maniac* was gone too.

There were two rescue divers in the helo. They were both former French SAS. Derek knew that because they were wearing T-shirts that said so. Derek asked, "There are a couple of Russians still alive. Are you gonna pick 'em up?"

"No," said the soldier. "They will be cared for by the village fishermen."

"Why not let the fishermen save me?" Derek asked.

"The Russians have an excuse to be here, you do not," sneered the Frenchman. Derek connected eyes with one of the drifting Russians. The Russian did the same. They remained locked on until the helo flew off.

Derek was more frightened over what would

happen next than he was in the water. The helo raced low over the reefs. There was no conversation.

In his head, Dell replayed the events of Avatoro over and over again, searching for the answer to the obvious question, what the hell went wrong? How did the Russians know about the attempted reading? Trawlers would not ordinarily have three military-grade Zodiacs on board, would they? The Russians had to have known Derek and Vela were coming. They were too well prepared. It crossed Derek's mind that they were set up.

The helo landed on a good-sized airfield where Derek saw several private jets parked. He did not know where he was. He was escorted by one of the Frenchmen to a waiting plane.

A uniformed woman and man were standing by the entry door on the tail side of the aircraft. "Good morning, Mr. Dell, I am Gina Bellavista and I'll be your captain today. This is Malcom Breckenridge. He is our co-pilot." Her accent was unmistakably American.

"Good day, Mr. Dell," said Malcom. "I'm friends with David Paxton. He sends his best regards and is delighted you are safe."

Derek said nothing. He managed to smile and nod in reply. The two pilots spoke as though they were flying some rich vacationer and not a traumatized contract diver.

Dell boarded the jet still wearing his peeled-back wetsuit. There sat Jensen Headman. Derek wondered how Jensen had arrived in French Polynesia so quickly after the Avatoro. He must have been there before the massive mess.

"Are you all right, mate?" asked Headman.

"Apart from my wrist I'm okay," Dell responded.

Jensen produced Derek's passport, the Sammy and a fresh change of clothing. Now Derek was really confused. Why did Headman have those items? They were left in Fiji, as always. Now, out of nowhere, Headman and Derek's personal stuff rocked up on a private jet in French Polynesia? What the hell? There were questions that needed answers.

Dell knew this gig was going to be different from the others. They covered the politics and risks in the pre-dive briefing in Maleqa. That said, he was not expecting this level of support. His fear increased. He did not escape from the Avatoro, he was being extracted. The difference frightened the hell out of Derek Dell.

"Sorry about Vela, mate," said Jensen. Derek nodded but remained silent. "I want you to know the set of protocols being used in this situation. We're headed to Fiji. We'll check into the Regent just as usual. Ratu Vunni will join us and we'll do a complete debriefing. Obviously, something went wrong and we need to find out what is was." Again, Derek remained silent and nodded his head in understanding. Headman continued, "After that, you will take the evening flight to LA then on to San Francisco. When you get home, we want you to lie low for a while. Keep the Sammy charged and properly chipped." Dell nodded in compliance.

Derek settled in for the ride to Fiji. He thought of Lydia and the impact this may have on her. Was she in danger? Did her dumbass Dad not only get Vela killed but put her in peril, too? There were so many questions, to few answers and so much guilt. One thing Dell knew for certain, he was in way over his head and he did not trust anyone.

The three men met in the privacy of Derek's room at the Regent. The debriefing did not last long. Derek meekly told the Avatoro story. He emphasized that the Russian preparation indicated they were expecting him and Vela. The Ratu looked over at Jensen with chagrin.

The Ratu and Headman had nothing to offer Derek in the way of explanation. They too had many unanswered questions. The meeting ended with the Ratu offering a prayer for Vela. All three lowered their heads.

Derek arrived at the Nadi Airport long before necessary to make the flight. He always flew first class so he checked in and went straight to the secluded first cabin lounge. Derek had been seen by the Russian sailors. He worried the airport could be watched even though he was now in Fiji. Such is the nature of paranoia.

On arrival in San Francisco he was greeted by Uncle Rico. Rico could tell Derek was completely exhausted. That was understandable for any international traveler. There was something else Rico noticed.

Rico was more like a parent to Derek than an uncle. Rico sensed further distress in his nephew. As they drove to Moss Beach Rico asked if there was something wrong, something he should know. Dell replied that there was some trouble. Possibly big trouble. He could not tell Rico the nature of the problems but asked for his help. Rico well knew the need for secrets. In Italy they called it "Omerta". This was the mafia vow of silence.

Rico lived only two blocks from where Dell's ex-wife Ann had settled. Lydia was with Ann during Dell's travels. Dell told Rico he was headed to Miracle Mountain Ranch for a while and wanted Rico to look after Lydia and Ann. Derek would call Ann and explain he had a mountain of work to do at the ranch and needed her to handle Lydia for a while.

They arrived in Moss Beach to the usual excited greeting from Wylie and Marco. The two dogs loved Derek so. Dell stashed his gear and called Ann and Lydia. With all the arrangements made, Derek grabbed the dogs and loaded the Blazer for the trip north to the ranch.

One item remained. Derek pulled a Beretta 9mm automatic handgun from the closet. He handed it to Rico and reiterated the need to protect Lydia and Ann. Rico handled the weapon as though he were its inventor. With hardly a glance, Rico ejected the clip, locked back the action and inspected the piece. Derek was surprised. It took a lot of practice to handle a gun like that. Derek didn't know if Rico was a guardian angel or, perhaps, his Ghost of Christmas Future. It didn't matter. Rico was the best man for Lydia's safety.

The drive to the ranch was difficult. Paranoia grew each mile along the way. Wylie and Marco were picking up on the vibe. They seemed on alert. Derek constantly scanned the rear-view mirror, looking for anything that seemed out of order. He knew he had to settle down a bit.

Arrival at the ranch was the usual. Excited dogs jumping from the Blazer, peeing everywhere and Nancy the manager, with a warm hello. Though cordial, Derek excused himself, blaming jet lag for his blown-out look. Bed was needed immediately. Nancy bought the story.

Derek hunkered down at MMR. Fear was in full blossom. He kept thinking of the American Wild West days. He imagined that every palm tree from Sydney to San Francisco had a "Wanted, Dead or Alive" poster hosting Derek's picture. The mind can be tricky, Derek thought.

Frequent calls to Rico soothed his concern over Lydia's safety. Lydia graduated from the Hamlin School and was now attending Branson. Branson was a private high school in Marin County. Ann convinced Derek they should rent a house in Mill Valley to lessen Lydia's commute to school. Dell thought this was a fantastic idea as it would be an additional layer of safety for his daughter. Ann was expecting push back as she did not know of Derek's predicament. The house was obtained.

At the ranch Derek engaged in setting up unusual security. His arsenal of guns and ammunition were a welcome sight for a frightened Dell. MMR was a tactical dream. The natural barriers of open space and steep ascent were complemented by two alert dogs and lots of firepower.

The set-up was perfect. Dell placed a power scoped 308 H&K sniper rifle on the deck off his bedroom. The pastures and road up to the house were in full sight from there. He strapped two AK-47s to the water tanks about one hundred feet above the housing area. The AK was Dell's favorite rifle. They could take anything. If a retreat battle ensued, he had firepower stashed.

Inside the house Derek hid handguns. A Desert Eagle .44 magnum sat in the umbrella bin next to the front door. A 10mm Smith and Wesson automatic and shoulder holster were on Dell at all times. He slept with three guns. An Uzi submachine gun, a long barrel Smith and Wesson revolver and a Streetsweeper automatic shotgun. A Gallil folding stock 308 unscoped sniper rifle was nearby. This was a heavy-duty gun that was so light Derek could run a great distance with it strapped to his back. Ammo depots were set up everywhere. Now, he had a recipe for a good night's sleep.

Dell's last concern was the fact that he had been seen by the Russian sailors who survived the Avatoro.

He was uncertain as to how good of look they may have gotten but his trepidation caused him to take action.

He had not eaten properly since Vela's death. He was losing weight quickly. Derek decided to continue the transformation of his body. He was never fat so losing a good deal of weight meant he had to decrease muscle mass. He knew exactly how to do that. Derek engaged his gym aggressively. He altered his training methods to reconfigure his body. Derek was dropping from two hundred thirty-five to one hundred eighty-five pounds.

Part of Dell's physical training included long distance running. To drop that weight, he had to put in several miles every day. The straight open roads surrounding the ranch were the perfect place to train. He could see any approaching vehicles from long distances. He always ran with the Smith and Wesson 10mm.

His long burnt-brown hair was now shorter and morphing over time to blond. He reckoned that the Russians — or anyone else — would not be looking for a lean, taut blond. Derek's comfort was slowly returning. At least he had a plan.

The Great Astrolabe Reef

As time passed Derek's fear became manageable. He remained concerned and a little paranoid but developed lifestyle alternatives that made him feel safe. He would meet up with Meg and the California Girls in different places. San Diego, San Francisco or perhaps at the Mill Valley house. Selecting a seat at restaurants where his back was not to the door became standard. Derek avoided being photographed and was always armed. His conduct was by no means a return to his desired normal life. It did, however, get him by.

His friends and business associates thought he was dying. Derek had lost so much weight they thought he was terminally ill. To show he was healthy and strong he entered and ran in the Fiji National Marathon. Dying men can't run over twenty-six miles in the tropics.

He frequently spoke with Ratu Vunni on the Sammy. There were no jobs planned as, frankly, technology was making Derek's trawler jobs obsolete. Their conversations were mostly helping Derek deal with the guilt he felt over Vela's death. Vunni questioned Derek on the details of Avatoro many times. In each instance Vunni pointed out that Derek did what Vela expected him to do. Vela was a soldier.

Derek spent most of his time at the ranch or in the Mill Valley house with Lydia. He never went to Moss Beach. He was too vulnerable there. The house sat empty.

At the ranch his tactical advantage was so strong that he slept well during this very troubling time. His arsenal of weapons certainly helped.

One day the Sammy rang. It was Ratu Vunni. There was a job to do. Vunni said that the specifics of the work were so critical that he would not discuss them on the phone, not even a Sammy with a secure chip. He wanted Derek on the first available plane to Fiji for a face-to-face.

Derek flatly turned Vunni down. He said he was done with contract diving and would not do another job. Vunni stressed the importance of the dive and reiterated his request that Derek take the job. Derek again declined. Vunni was very disappointed.

Derek Dell was now using the world wide web and communicating with people via email. He was sitting at the ranch one day with the Smith and Wesson strapped on and an AK 47 by his chair. He was on the laptop computer looking at emails. He found one from a college friend named Vanessa. She was a fraternity little sister and a good pal of Derek's. Vanessa had married Derek's friend Jim. He was one of those good-looking football guys. Derek liked them both very much.

Vanessa's email was sent to everyone in her

contacts. She was a school teacher in Sacramento. Her email told of the garden she was filling and the joy it would bring as the flowers bloomed. Derek was envious. He had wanted to be a gardener since he was a child. Vegetables, flowers and fruit were all on his hope list. Derek admired Vanessa's life. Vanessa was living the dream Derek had never known.

At this point Derek's despair had been affecting him for a long time. The email from Vanessa made something snap in his head. He had reached the tipping point where fear turns into anger, anger turns into courage, and courage turns into action. Derek had, at last, focused past his fear. He called Vunni and said he would take the job.

On the plane to Fiji Derek pondered how he would end this part of his career. Maybe technology would do the job. Possibly the Cold War would just end. He did not know. He wondered how the job Vunni spoke of could be so secret he wouldn't discuss it by phone. There were a lot of unknowns. He would have the answers soon. The plane was descending into Nadi Airport.

The routine was the same. A lean blond Derek checked in at the Regent. After another fabulous buffet breakfast, he headed to the pool for a tan and a rest. Ratu Vunni would be coming to the resort for dinner with Derek. Dead Dave was joining in. Derek looked forward to seeing them both. They had not been together since the Avatoro disaster several months ago. Derek wondered why Jensen Headman was not coming to dinner. Dell had grown to like that guy, even though he was a piss stain on the pants of New Zealand.

Later that evening Dell was dressing for dinner. They were dining in the finest restaurant at the resort. A little class was required. Derek selected Armani slacks and a silk Aloha shirt, his preferred tropical business garb. The shoes were Prada casual loafers. He waited for Ratu Vunni and Dead Dave in the bar.

Vunni turned up in a formal sulu, jacket and tie. Dead Dave, like Derek, chose slacks and shirt. Neither man could recognize Derek. His weight loss and blond hair threw them off.

It was clear all three men were delighted to see one another. The handshakes turned into embraces. Their eye contact was solid and their excitement sincere. They sat and ordered drinks.

Derek asked how Marinea and the kids were doing. Vunni put him at ease and said they were fine. Vela had left a tidy sum and Marinea would live her remaining life in comfort and security. There were even sufficient funds to send the children to New Zealand for school. Derek was so pleased.

A tuxedoed Maître D' approached the table where the three men sat. He spoke to Ratu Vunni in Fijian. Derek understood enough to know that the private room Vunni had organized for dinner was ready.

They adjourned to the restaurant. The private room was lovely. It was often used for wedding parties and the like. Flowers and art work were everywhere. The guys were most comfortable. Vunni did not drink alcohol but Derek and Dead Dave ordered some darn good Australian wine. A fabulous Caesar salad was prepared at the table. Derek's main meal was fish (walu) and vegetables. These days that was his primary diet.

Dinner finished, coffee was served and the Fijian staff vanished at the snap of Vunni's fingers. It was time to get down to business.

Vunni took control. Ratu insisted that Dead Dave and Derek promise their silence on this meeting. Confidentiality was vital. The two kavelaqi agreed. He said there was going to be trouble in Fiji. Another military coup was planned in a few months. It would happen after the turn of the millennium, in early 2000. Derek said, "Not another coup. How many does that make now? Four?" In actual fact, he did not remember. All three men had lived or worked in Fiji for years. The country struggled with its independence and the formation of a written constitution. Coups were part of that struggle.

Ratu Vunni continued. The worry was that a Russian trawler was anticipated in Fijian waters about the same time. It was going to be fishing the waters off the Great Astrolabe Reef in the south of Fiji. The vulnerability of the government during a coup is quite delicate. Russia is a predator country. Vunni did not want them in his waters, particularly during a coup.

Derek inquired, "How does this dive differ from the others? Can't we use the Kiribati template?" Vunni confessed that there were two major differences. First, this job was not funded as of yet. Derek asked, "Is that why Jensen isn't here?" Vunni nodded. The second issue was the sensitive matter.

Ratu Vunni did not want Derek to read the trawler with a karlmalden. Vunni was not at all worried that a suitcase bomb would be delivered in Suva. Vunni wanted Derek to disable the trawler. Vunni wanted to send a message that Russia could not play their game in Fiji as they had done in Vanuatu, Kiribati and elsewhere. Vunni did not want his beloved Fiji manipulated by the Russians. Derek sensed this was quite personal with Vunni.

Derek asked the obvious question: what was meant by "disable the trawler?". Derek reiterated his conviction that he did not want to injure anyone and surely would not kill anybody. Dead Dave asked, "What do you mean, you don't want to hurt or kill anybody? What the hell do you call the Avatoro?"

Dell bristled over Dead Dave's comment. "Look," Dell said, "I meant I would not INTENTIONALLY hurt or kill anyone." Everyone knew they were in a dangerous business. That's why the money was so good.

Vuni put their minds at ease. There was no intent to harm anyone. Derek would dive alone and it would be brief. He was to descend as usual past two hundred feet. Avoiding detection, fishing nets and gear was, of course, vital. He would ascend and place four small explosives near the trawler's rudder and prop. The charges were light and would only disable the power mechanism, rendering the trawler dead in the water.

This was quite a change from the Kiribati template. In fact, Dell thought this was an act of war. He worried that he would end up as some sort of criminal sought by Interpol, or worse. He also voiced concern that he would be detected. An American getting caught doing something like this would be politically disastrous.

Vunni agreed. There was great risk in this job. Not so much the physical danger but political and criminal risk. Vunni pointed out that unless a significant message was sent, the trawler presence could lead to a Russian/Fijian fishing treaty like the others. Fishing treaties lead to military bases and nuclear missile silos.

Derek was more concerned that a Russian/Fijian treaty would result in him being identified as the boatman from Avatoro. Vunni never discovered how the Russians were tipped off about the Avatoro. Derek could not live in fear for the rest of his life. It was time to end this business and keep the Russians out of Fiji. Derek agreed to do the job but insisted this would be the last.

There was one more change. Derek told Vunni to send the nitrox regulator and oxygen analyzer to California in the diplomatic pouch as usual. When Derek returned the pouch to Fiji it would contain Derek's Smith and Wesson 44. Dead Dave asked, "You mean that Dirty Harry gun you bought for the Arctic dives?"

"Mine is cooler than Dirty Harry's," joked Dell. "I've got African burl wood grips and nickel plating."

Vunni asked, if Derek did not want to hurt anyone, why bring a weapon? Derek answered that, after the Avatoro, he did not want to engage in any Zodiac chases. He wanted to be able to shoot the pontoons out of any Russian pursuers. There was no passage or land that far off the Astrolabe Reef. If the Russians gave chase they would certainly catch Derek.

Last was the matter of funding. Vunni had no deep pockets flowing from Jensen Headman on this job. He did, however, have a plan. The Olympic Games were in Sydney in 2000. It was a big deal all over the South Pacific. Vunni planned to convince Jensen that a karlmalden reading was necessary to protect the Sydney Games from the dangers of a suitcase bomb. The trawler was in the area and the job would not cost much. It was a sound precaution. Jensen would not be told of the plans to disable the trawler. All three men thought funding would be a cinch.

The three closed by offering a toast to Vela.

Derek left Fiji with plans to return for the final contract dive. There were only a few months for planning details. He was now fifty years old.

The Final Dive

Derek entered himself in the Fiji National Marathon scheduled in April of 2000. Because of the Olympics in Sydney there were many world-class runners entered in the race. He knew of the planned coup and was sure the race would not be run. It was, however, important he establish his presence in Western Fiji.

He landed at Nadi Airport a few days before the race and checked in at the Regent. Instead of then heading to the pool Derek took a cab to Lautoka. He was meeting Dead Dave and seeing the new *Maniac 3*. They were not flying the Nomad this time. The Astrolabe Reef was too close to use a plane that big. A smaller aircraft had been organized. The *Maniac 3* would ride outside the plane between the landing pontoons. Derek did not like this arrangement but Dead Dave was confident. That was enough for Dell. It was a short flight.

Dead Dave arrived before Derek. He greeted Dell with an unusually broad smile. The reason became apparent when they opened the warehouse door. The *Maniac 3* was revealed.

On the surface it looked like the other *Maniac*s. Since the budget for aircraft had been reduced, more money was available for the *Maniac*. The fuel cell had been increased in size to offer far greater range. This could be valuable if things went bad and Dead Dave flew off. Derek could make it to land or "out-gas" any pursuit.

More importantly, the engine size had been increased and the horsepower jumped substantially. Every available racing boat part was used on this version of the *Maniac*. Dell was delighted. This was the kind of boat he was hoping for. "Cheap bastards should have juiced this boat years ago," Derek lamented. "Vela might still be alive."

The warehouse door opened. It was Ratu Vunni, with two of his tactical staff. Derek and Dead Dave greeted them warmly. The team was assembled.

The details of the next evening's job were discussed. As usual, Vunni would handle command. General strategy was designed by him.

Final execution and job details were up to Dead Dave and Derek. Dead Dave's part was pretty simple as the Astrolabe was close. Ad-libbing, disregard for sanity and other non-conforming violations were, of course, left to Derek.

The team addressed the disabling process to be used on the trawler. Derek was understandably nervous about handling any type of underwater explosive. Even weak, non-lethal charges bothered him. He had never done anything like this before. Derek was the only non-military man on the team.

Vunni's staff officer Timoce (Timothy) took the floor. He produced one of the devices from a duffle. It was relatively simple in appearance. Timoce explained that the device contained a tiny bit of C-4. This was a plastique explosive developed by the Americans. It was directional and attached to the trawler magnetically. A covered toggle switch was located dead center on the outer side. All Dell had to do was uncover the switch and throw it. The timer would begin count down. He had two and a half minutes before detonation. Dell was advised to get far away and surface to minimize any unintended impact from the small blast. Though there was likely no physical risk from the mini charge, Derek's ears could be injured. Sound travels effectively underwater.

There were four devices. Dell would place them on the ship's power substructure: prop, drive shaft, rudder and the like. The rest was straight out of the Kiribati template. Swim back to the *Maniac*, over to Dead Dave and fly off.

The trawler's crew would be busy dealing with the problem. In the confusion and activity Derek could easily slip away. No one worried too much about detection. Moreover, the cover of darkness was on their side.

Vunni hauled out the diplomatic pouch Derek had sent down by DHL. He handed it to Derek, saying, "Your nitrox gear and ridiculous pistol are here. You will be picked up at nine p.m. tomorrow night." The meeting ended.

Dead Dave drove Derek back to the Regent. Dell had the remainder of the day and all of the next to ponder what he was about to do.

Derek hit the pool for some sun and rest. A great setting to sort out this job in his mind. He figured that the coup was their best cover. The Russians would surely blame the Fijians for any maritime skullduggery. No one would think differently. The hope was that Moscow would view the incident as a small statement of rejection by the Republic of Fiji.

It would also remind the Russians of their vulnerability. If your opposition can actually touch you, there is a clear and present risk. This was the statement Vunni wanted to make. Derek reckoned he was merely delivering a kiss from the people of Fiji. In its own way this strategy was very South Pacific. The peaceful nature of South Pacific people was ingrained in this plan. Instead of injury or death, only a strong message would be sent.

Dell had sufficiently diminished the gravity of this job in his mind to allow him some comfort with his duties.

There was a bustle among the staff at the pool bar. The excited barman was speaking only in Fijian. Derek understood enough to know that the coup had just set off. The military had taken control of the Parliament House in the capital city of Suva.

Derek was sitting in an area with other runners who had signed up for the Fiji National Marathon. Word of the coup spread quickly through the resort. Families on holiday, marathoners and other foreign visitors began to worry. Dell envisioned the diver cancellations Aqua Trek would be receiving.

Derek began to ponder his worst-case scenario. He couldn't imagine getting caught. The trawler crew would simply have to focus on the ship and damage control. They would not h02ave the opportunity to chase Derek. He was certain of that. With the hyped-up *Maniac 3 he* would be home free once he got to it. If he had to, he could just run the *Maniac* full speed until he hit Kadavu (Kandavu). It was the closest island to the Astrolabe. Confidence set in.

The post-dive plan was something Derek had looked forward to for a very long time. Dead Dave would return Derek to the Regent in time to run the marathon in the morning. The day after the race Derek would head on to Tahiti. Meg and the California Girls were meeting him in Papeete for a holiday at the Bora Bora Hotel. Dell would have two days alone prior to their arrival. He was sure he could pull himself together before then.

Derek Dell had hopes and dreams just like anyone else. After this job he would be done with contract diving. At fifty years of age he began to think of his future and retirement. He envisioned his garden, his lifelong desire for the simplicity and peace it could offer. It seemed that Derek had finally had his fill of adventure. Perhaps in Bora Bora with Meg and the California Girls he could find his way to a normal, peaceful existence. He slept well that night.

The following morning Derek had breakfast with several other runners. They were a great group of people who had trained hard for either the Sydney Olympics or the small Fijian race. Derek always admired athletes. This bunch were all better than him. Derek was pretty sure the race would be cancelled. He certainly didn't want to return from the midnight dive and have to run a twenty-six mile stretch in the morning.

The group went to the pool after they ate. The day before a marathon, runners are advised to hydrate and rest. They decided to sit in the shade by the pool sipping Fiji water most of the day. The evening meal should be a carbo load. Derek always chose spaghetti.

Later that morning the marathon officials journeyed to the pool with final news of the race. The event was on! They shortened the distance to only twelve miles and it would be run entirely on Denarau Island and the Regent grounds. Derek was disappointed. He wanted to avoid running the damn race but felt he could manage a mere twelve miles. After all, the dive would be brief and, if all went well, he would be back at the Regent by one-thirty a.m.

Around nine p.m. Derek grabbed his dive bag and left the room. He avoided the lobby and walked to the road via the golf course. Dead Dave was waiting in a van.

There was little conversation on the drive to Lautoka. It was obvious both men were nervous. Just before they arrived Dead Dave took his eyes off the road and met Derek's. Dave said, "Before we set out on this mission, I just wanted to say that it has been a pleasure soldiering with you these past few years." Derek was honored to be included in Dead Dave's circle of soldiers. In the past much had been made of the fact Derek was not military. The two shook hands.

When they arrived at the dockside warehouse Timoce already had the *Maniac* in the water. The engine started on the first pull, a good sign.

Timoce called to Derek and Dead Dave. They shut down the *Maniac* and walked back into the warehouse. Timoce produced a backpack which contained the small charges. Derek examined the devices to ensure he was comfortable with their mechanics.

The diver and pilot boarded the *Maniac* and headed to the aircraft.

On the plane Derek again checked every piece of equipment. The oxygen level in his tank was perfect and all gear was present and working. Dead Dave fired the aircraft engine and the two taxied out.

The flight toward the trawler seemed endless. Derek's nerves were sparking. He knew that his angst would subside once he hit the water. It always did.

Finally they arrived at the Astrolabe. The skies were cloudy. It rained a lot in this part of Fiji. Derek was pleased. The dim conditions would cloak his dive.

After a few minutes search Dead Dave located the Russians. Both men took compass readings. Dead Dave banked off and sought the best landing site.

They were a long way off the reef. In fact, they were in international waters and technically not even in Fiji. Too late to ponder politics and law. Both men were focused on the job.

Derek released the *Maniac* from its goofball rigging between the pontoons of the aircraft. The boat fared well on the short flight.

He raced off toward the lights of the trawler. The weight of the heavy pistol shoved in Derek's wetsuit and the C-4 backpack meant he needed no weight belt on the dive.

Derek drift anchored the *Maniac* as close to the trawler as possible. After submerging beneath the choppy waters, he discovered the visibility was dreadful. All conditions were favorable.

The trawler was lit up like a spacecraft. There were underwater lights as well. Derek had no problem locating the hull during his ascent from deep water.

Clutching the backpack to his chest Derek continued his ascent. The poor visibility under the boat empowered the diver. Any cameras would be useless in the turbid mess.

He swam the length of the boat groping to located the power train and rudder. This was taking too long. He had to increase his pace.

Derek's breathing rate increased. Air was going quickly.

Finally locating the mechanics of the trawler, he hastily mounted the explosives. Unsure the best spots had been selected, he had to move quickly. All the toggle switches were thrown at the same time.

The *Maniac* was sitting off the port side of the

trawler. After dropping back to depth Derek hastily swam toward the boat. As soon as possible he surfaced. Derek did not want to be underwater when the small blast took place. Even a firecracker pop underwater could cause hearing problems.

Derek reached the surface to the sound of outboard engines roaring at full throttle. He had thoughts of the Avatoro. They were headed toward the *Maniac* off their port side. Derek did not know what to do. The unmistakable feeling in his stomach signaled panic was setting in.

He decided to reverse his direction and swim off the starboard side of the trawler.

Dell heard excited radio chatter but, regrettably, did not speak Russian. He had a pretty good idea that the Russian Zodiac had discovered the *Maniac*. His fears were confirmed when he heard the unmistakable sound of an AK-47 shredding his brand-new boat.

Despite the severity of the situation Derek could not help but think, Damn, I only had around a half hour in that boat. Vunni will be pissed. The third *Maniac* sank in thousands of feet of water.

Derek was certain Dead Dave would fly off at the sound of the AK. His suspicions were correct.

He had no idea what would happen next but was anxiously waiting for the charges to go off. At least the Russians would have to deal with a damaged craft. It seemed so long that Derek questioned if the charges were going to ignite at all.

The Russian Zodiac was headed back to its mother

ship. Derek remained on the surface off the starboard side. Where were the damn blasts? he thought.

An incredibly powerful spotlight pierced through the night from the starboard side of the trawler. Derek ducked underwater to escape their notice.

The Russians had located his bubbles with the powerful light. He heard another AK open fire. Fear rumbled through Dell as he watched the bullets penetrate the water near his bubble trail. Where in hell were those blasts? he wondered.

Dell decided to ditch his gear and swim away from the bubble trail. Hopefully the Russians would continue shooting in that direction.

That move worked pretty well as both the searchlight and gunfire followed the bubbles of Derek's abandon gear. He was now about ten feet underwater, holding his breath. The searchlight soon peered in his direction. The bubble trail was gone.

Derek was no longer afraid. He was so focused on his dilemma there was no room for emotion.

It did not appear that the charges were going to work. The Russian light searched the water just above Derek's head. He could no longer hold his breath.

Derek drew the pistol from his wetsuit, headed to the surface and began firing at the searchlight. Without fear, his aim was not hindered by emotions. Still, it took three rounds to hit the damn spotlight.

Dell spun, tucked the gun away and started swimming for his life. He wanted to get as far away from the trawler as possible. Locating him would be more difficult with distance.

His strong kick came in handy. Surfacing for a breath of air then descending for the swim was a rhythm that worked well in the murky chop. This was Derek's coveted A game.

He saw the sky flare brightly. Lightning was preceding a rain storm, so he thought. An instant later the sea exploded with such a furious sound that the trailing vibration threw Derek up and out of the water.

He splashed down in a state of shock. Derek raised his head in time to see the trawler completely obliterated by explosion. There were several blasts which tore the boat mercilessly apart. At one point, parts of the craft exploded again when they were already in the air. The boat continued to blow up. It seemed that there wasn't a piece of the Russian trawler left that was any bigger than Derek's hand.

In his mind Derek had already given himself up for dead. He began to enjoy the colorful concussions of the Russian trawler's demise. He chuckled as he wondered who screwed up, or perhaps, who set him up.

He knew a blast of that size would summon every shark in the area. Deep water hunters would be very large. He pondered his likely end.

Derek sat on the surface, waiting in thought. He heard an engine in the distance. A fishing boat might be in the area. Perhaps he would be saved. Now somewhat energized, his ears sharpened for another hint of sound.

It was not a boat at all. Derek saw the lights of an aircraft flying above him. It had to be Dead Dave. The plane landed and started a taxi search for Derek.

After a few minutes Dead Dave heard Dell yelling. The two met up.

It is difficult to explain the feeling of going from submission to the probability of death to the jubilation of being saved. Derek was in that space.

Dead Dave helped Derek onto the plane. Dell's ears were bleeding from the blast. His hearing would surely suffer.

"Thanks, man," was all Derek uttered. He was certainly in shock. Dead Dave flew off like a scalded cat.

Once they were clear of the Astrolabe, Derek inquired why Dead Dave had returned. Dave explained that Ratu Vunni ordered him to do so. After Dave had informed Vunni that the trawler was demolished there was no risk of discovery or capture. Clearly there were no Russians left alive. No one to report anything to Moscow or anyone else. Derek remained silent for the duration of the flight.

Ratu Vunni was waiting in the Lautoka dockside warehouse. He brought a doctor to examine Derek. Since the *Maniac* was lost, the boys had to swim from the plane to the dock.

Derek was settling down emotionally. The doctor declared Dell would be fine. The tensions in the room were relaxing.

Derek inquired, "Ratu Vunni, what the hell happened out there? Those charges were designed to sink that ship, not disable it! Who set me up?" Vunni had no answer. He was as surprised as Derek. The look on Vunni's face said he told the truth.

The devices were American. Were they behind all this? Getting the Fijians to do their dirty work? Did the Americans know of Derek Dell? There were many more questions and none of them had answers.

The men decided to follow the plan. Derek made Vunni promise to return his pistol in the diplomatic pouch. Vunni agreed.

Dead Dave drove Derek back to the Regent. They were all confused and wondering how this mess would play out. Dell was happy with the plan. As soon as the marathon was over, he would head off to Tahiti on the evening Air New Zealand flight. Derek was, in the end, just happy to be alive.

His appearance in the next day's run was an important part of his alibi. Derek finished the race dead last. Even a guy in a wheelchair beat him.

It wasn't until he was on the ANZ plane to Tahiti that he began to relax. Shivers occasionally traversed his spine. He was exiting shock.

Derek examined every option. Was he in danger from the Americans? Was he a loose end? He fired a damn gun at a Soviet ship. Then blew it up! Was that an act of war? Perhaps terrorism? At least, it was an act of piracy. There were still no answers.

Dell never wanted to hurt anyone. Between the

Avatoro and this mess he had certainly missed that goal. To his surprise he didn't feel guilty. After all, Dead Dave said Dell was a soldier. Soldiers understood the ways of battle. Derek decided not to bullshit himself further. He was no soldier and he felt terrible about the men who died.

The long flight allowed Derek time to reason things out. There was no-one to tell what had happened. All hands went down. Even if a message was sent to Moscow, what would it say? Did they see a bulky brown-haired boatman from the Avatoro or a lean blond on the Astrolabe? Did they see anyone at all? At best, he would just be a ghost. Derek felt the Russians were in check.

The Americans were also cornered. There was no way in hell they would associate with this event. Any reprisals on Derek would have to be explained. After all, Derek was an American citizen. If the Americans were involved, they did not want any light shone on this matter.

It was hoped the Fijians would be blamed. After all, Derek was pretty sure that is what Vunni wanted. The rebels behind the coup would be happy to take credit. Possibly the Fijian Navy would want the prize?

Most probably, the entire matter would be swept under the rug and defined as a horrible fishing boat accident. That was the true nature of Cold War politics.

Derek arrived in Papeete around one a.m. By the time he cleared customs and transferred to the

Sheraton it was past two. The bars were closed for the night. Derek went to bed.

Sleep was his friend that night. Emotional and physical exhaustion often leads to a deep slumber. Dell rose the following morning with a clear head and quite rested. He donned his sulu (or pareo, as called in Tahiti).

He pondered the morality of the Astrolabe gig. Derek had been highly manipulated and he did not know by whom. The lives that were lost were probably lost in vain. This was the type of thing that made the Cold War such a dishonorable clash. There were no heroes or known acts of bravery. Mostly a bunch of secret acts played out by a bunch of secret people.

Every soldier believes God is on their side. The problem is that the other side feels the same. There was no morality to war. Some feel war is fought for patriotism and freedom. Any soldier will tell you that war is fought for the man next to you in the fox hole. In battle it is your brother beside you that inspires your bravery.

His morning philosophical moment would have to wait. Derek needed coffee. He grabbed the room service menu.

Derek was starved. He ordered breakfast and gobbled his fill. Dell opened the door to his deck overlooking the pool. Feeling better, he sat and sipped coffee. Dell continued to wonder whether his act on the Astrolabe was that of an angel or a demon. Meg and the California Girls would arrive in two days. He must have his head straight or Lydia would surely sense that something was not right.

Dell was a believer in signs born of the universe. He would interpret any small indicator in the most positive light. This often helped him justify his actions.

While sitting on his deck with coffee he noticed three ladies setting up by the pool. In Tahiti women frequently are topless in their swim gear. Such was the case with these three angels. They were very attractive.

Derek moved straight to the pool to make their acquaintance. As it turned out, there was a black pearl convention at the hotel. The girls were booth models from LA.

Nonetheless, Derek took the event as a sign. If God sent him three gorgeous angels he must have been on Derek's side in the Astrolabe.

A simple, foolish conclusion born of lust was exactly what Derek needed to justify his acts. He had the Astrolabe in check.

Derek spent the next two days enjoying the attributes of Papeete and the company of the booth models. They turned out to be fun kids but were way too young for Derek. He took a fatherly role. Everyone had a good time.

When Meg and the California Girls arrived, Derek Dell came alive. He knew his career in contract diving had ended. This holiday with Lydia would be more precious than ever. Derek had a chance. He might finally achieve the peaceful life he wanted so badly.

A Cook's Bay Tragedy

Derek Dell's struggle for life in Cook's Bay was coming to an end. His life had flashed before his eyes and the old man now lay motionless beneath the water. His brain no longer darted through the past and his heartbeat was slowing.

Drake and Charlie were topside, looking over the pontoon of the *Maniac 4*. Drake saw blood coming from the area of Derek's lobster dive. He instructed Charlie to stay with the boat, then quickly donned his mask snorkel and fins. Drake splashed into the water to view Derek with clarity offered by the dive mask. He could see Derek was hurt badly. Blood was everywhere.

Frantic, Drake attempted to descend to Derek and pull him from the deep. Each time, Drake could not clear his ears and was unable to dive deep enough to reach Derek. Blood was now oozing from both of Drake's ears.

Drake heard a splash. From the corner of his eye he saw Charlie descending like an arrow. With no mask or snorkel, Charlie used only fins to kick his way past his dad and on to Poppy below.

Charlie's hand gripped firmly on Poppy's tank valve. The rookie snorkeler and his grandpa began to ascend. As Derek neared the surface the air in his BC expanded, lessening Charlie's upward struggle.

At the surface Drake and Charlie dumped Derek's gear and wrestled the old man onto the boat. Poppy was alive. He uttered one phrase. "Sea snakes."

Drake called Juliet for instructions and started the engines of the *Maniac 4*. Juliet was still in Papeete with the girls. She remained calm and explained to Drake that she would have a doctor meet them at C-bay in a few moments. She asked if Drake was comfortable finding the house from the ocean. Drake replied he was already at full speed and could see the C-bay beach.

Drake ran the *Maniac* up on shore. He and Charlie helped Poppy from the boat and into bed. The medical team showed up quickly. South Pacific medical facilities routinely keep anti-venom on hand. Sea snake bites occur frequently. The doctor was more concerned over the eel bite than the sea snakes. Stitches were in order.

The doctor asked Drake how long Derek had been underwater. Drake answered that the entire dive was only seven minutes. Drake had set his watch when Derek splashed down and only seven minutes had expired. Drake further offered that only about three minutes had expired before he sighted Derek's blood in the water.

Derek sat slowly up and said, "Only seven minutes? Really? It seemed like a lifetime to me."